The Secret Company In Hidden Valley

A suspense novel written by

Mary Howard

Mary Howard

Published by Mary Howard

Copyright © 2011 Mary Howard

All rights reserved.

ISBN: 978-0-9812930-1-1

Website: www.TheSecretCompanyBook.com

To: Chloe, Kurt, and Simon

CHAPTER 1

It was dawn on a spring day. The temperature hovered around the freezing mark. A thick layer of mist floated a few feet above the ground. Golden rays from the morning sun were beginning to light up the plains of Hidden Valley. Shadows on the surrounding hills made the valley appear like the huge nest of a giant pre-historic bird.

Greenvale was a small city located in the center of the valley. Known as a perfect getaway place, it attracted a large number of visitors every year.

Along the cobblestone sidewalks of Greenvale's downtown core were decorated store windows, colorful striped awnings, antique gas-lit lamps, and numerous cafés with outdoor patios.

In the downtown core, the train station did great business during the summer months making daily round-trips to Bayport, one hundred and fifty miles due-west of Greenvale.

At the north end of the valley was the sprawling campus of Dale University. Built sixty years ago on a prime piece of wooded land, the university was the focal point for higher education in the valley district. Each year two thousand students made a pilgrimage from all parts of the country to attend classes there. Several of the university's professors had received grants from prestigious organizations and were often publicly recognized for the research work they did.

Greenvale was frequently the hub of secret conferences, often arranged via the Internet, which drew strangers together on a mission. It was considered an ideal place to plan projects because of its remote location, not to mention the high level of oxygen in the valley air which proved to be an intellectual stimulant.

A twin-engine plane began circling the circumference of the valley preparing for an early-morning landing at Pineview Airport. Red lights on the wing tips flashed on and off as the plane made its smooth descent. After chirping down on the narrow airport strip, the plane slowed to a stop near the tiny terminal building. Four passengers disembarked as well as a two-man crew. After collecting their luggage, they walked briskly towards the terminal.

*　　*　　*

At nine o'clock in the morning, on the first day of April, the students at Dale University were either taking their final exams or studying for them. As a result, the hallway in the administrative building was empty.

Professor Peter Preston sauntered down the hallway and stopped in front of the conference room door. He was there to attend a meeting with the university's board of directors. He had a vague uneasy feeling that made him reluctant to enter the room. It was the kind of feeling some people might refer to as a premonition of something bad to come.

What's making me nervous? Peter mildly wondered. Shrugging off the sensation, he opened the door and walked into the room.

Wood paneling on the lower half of the walls made the room

2

gloomy. Except for the furniture, the room was bare of adornments. There were no pictures on the walls. There was no carpet on the floor.

Professor Preston walked immediately to a vacant chair placed in front of the boardroom table. *I guess this is meant for me.* He sat down and set his briefcase beside the chair. Folding his hands in his lap, he began to wait for the meeting to commence.

Professor Preston was in his early forties, five-foot-ten, with wavy light-brown hair, and in good physical shape. He wore his usual conservative attire: a navy jacket, beige pants, and a white shirt accessorized by a silver tie.

Peter Preston had been a professor at Dale University for twelve years. He was one of eight professors in the *Computers & Technology* department. As well as teaching a full course load, he was the university's Internet consultant and web-designer.

The professor could guess what this meeting was going to be about. He had been to other similar ones before. In his opinion they could all be summed up in two of the most dreaded words in business: *budget cuts!*

His department had already been affected by budget cuts in several ways. For instance, whenever he sent a requisition to the admin department asking for new office furniture, the requisition invariably came back with a large stamp on it saying: NOT APPROVED. The reason was always the same; the budget would not allow for unnecessary expenses.

As if office furniture isn't necessary, Peter would quietly grumble on these occasions. And then last November the dean casually suggested an evening class be added to Professor Preston's curriculum. "You won't mind, will you, professor?"

As if he had a choice!

Who could he go to and file a complaint? Not the dean, obviously. Not the board of trustees. Not a union. The answer was: *no one*. Reluctantly Peter learned to work around the budget cuts, adapt to them the best he could, and keep his complaints to himself.

It bothered him that budget cuts always seemed to be unilateral decisions. Why didn't the board ever ask the staff for their opinions? The practice of forcing budget cuts onto the staff, without consulting them first, vaguely insulted Peter's intelligence.

As he waited, he began to sense this time it might be something more serious than a budget cut. He surmised they wouldn't bring a panel of five directors together just to ask him to fill in for another professor who was going away on a vacation. They were up to something. He could feel it in the air.

Would he lose his secretary this time? Would he have to take a cut in pay? He hoped not.

The panel of five directors sat behind a polished boardroom table made of cherry wood. Two of them were from the board of trustees. The other two were retired professors — Professor Winston and Professor Beam. In the center sat Dan Wilcox, the dean of Dale University.

The directors were discussing something amongst themselves in hushed tones while they sifted through a stack of papers they had prepared for the meeting. There was nervousness in their mannerisms which only added to the mounting tension in the room. Occasionally one of them would glance up at Professor Preston as though plotting their strategy on how to break the bad news to him.

Dan Wilcox looked up from his notes, peered over his bifocal glasses, and studied Professor Preston for a moment. The dean was in his mid-sixties, showing only slight signs of aging. He considered himself the lord of his domain. He assumed everyone who worked at the university would be just as enthusiastic about its progress as he was.

Dan Wilcox said, "Professor Preston!"

The professor jumped in his chair slightly, adjusted his tie, but didn't answer.

"As you may or may not be aware, Professor Preston, many universities are participating in a new program called Career Focus."

Professor Preston frequently heard about programs the university was involved in, however this was one he had not yet heard about. Saying nothing, he simply gave the dean a small tight smile.

The dean continued. "Career Focus was developed by the Professional Careers Association, whose founder is a fellow by the name of Benjamin Bright. We hope to achieve two basic goals with this new program. The first goal is to allow students a chance to specialize in a career from the onset of their post-secondary education — rather than making them wait until graduate studies, as is the present method."

Dan Wilcox paused for a moment to take a sip of ice water from a glass in front of him.

"The second goal of Career Focus is to make our universities — how shall I politely say this — more lucrative."

Professor Preston agreed with the dean that these were worthwhile goals. How would they be achieved?

The dean leaned forward eagerly in his chair. "Under the directives of Career Focus each university is required to choose its own specialty. That university will then teach only courses geared towards achieving degrees relating to that particular field of study.

"Once a student chooses their career, they must match it up with the appropriate university that would allow them to fulfill their goals.

"For example, Dale University has chosen to specialize in Environmental Studies. We chose this specialty largely due to our superb natural surroundings."

The dean swept his hand towards the floor-to-ceiling windows behind Professor Preston where a copse of pine trees could easily be seen. The dean was right about the presence of nature. Surrounding the university were wildlife in abundance and an amazing variety of trees and shrubs. Any astute ecology student could easily identify at least one hundred different botanical life-forms. It was the perfect setting for a budding earth-scientist.

The dean continued, "This means, beginning next semester, all students who attend Dale University will take ecology courses only. Consequently, we will be closing all departments that do *not* relate to Environmental Studies. One of the departments we plan to close is — unfortunately for you, professor — Computers & Technology."

Was there a hint of a smile on the dean's face? Professor Preston sucked in his breath. Close his department?!! Did he just hear the dean correctly? This was no budget cut. They are going to cancel his position altogether! What could he do to stop it?

"Is this decision final?" Professor Preston blurted out, half-rising from his seat.

"Ah ... yes ... I'm afraid so."

Professor Winston sensed the mood in the room changing and quickly interjected. "We have drawn up a list of several universities who *will* be specializing in technology. You are eligible to apply for a position at any of these institutions. We have written up a Letter of Recommendation providing details of your excellent performance here at Dale University. This should help you get a better job offer. Be sure to include a copy of this letter with your C.V. when you send out employment applications."

Employment applications? Peter could feel a heat begin to build under his skin.

Leaning forward, Professor Winston handed the agitated professor a red pocket-style folder secured with a piece of string.

Donald Banks, the youngest of the directors, pitched in with, "And please accept our sincerest apologies!"

All the members quickly nodded in agreement. Yes, apologies were in order.

"Thanks," mumbled Professor Preston, although he wasn't sure if that was the appropriate response or not. But at least it wasn't the one that came immediately to mind. Pulling his reading glasses out of his inside jacket pocket, he snapped them open and put them on. He began to glance over the papers.

While Professor Preston scanned the documents, the dean lightly drummed his fingers on the table. Obviously he wanted this meeting to be done and over with. Who could blame him? Dismissing personnel must rank high on the list of stress-related activities — even when it came accompanied with an appropriate excuse.

The dean wasn't without sympathy for the professor losing his post at Dale University. His heart ached for all the professors who were in the same spot. He said in a generous voice, "As our way of compensating you for your lost post here at Dale University, Professor Preston, we will be providing you with a full-year salary as severance pay. This payment, as well as other benefits you are entitled to receive, will be available at the Cashier's Office on the first day of August. A list of these payments is included in your folder there." He waved a finger in the general direction of the red folder.

Professor Beam began to explain to Peter about an option to transfer his pension fund to the institution where his new post would be. "Dale University has an agreement with all the institutions participating in Career Focus. You will not lose any funds accumulated in your pension so far. All you need to do is let us know where your new post will be ... and the transfer arrangements will be made."

What a bonus! Peter thought sarcastically and glared at Beam before continuing to glance absent-mindedly over the documents.

The dean casually asked, "Do you have any questions?"

Questions? Professor Preston could barely breathe as he looked up at the dean. What he had were more like comments! He felt furious. He had come to the meeting prepared for another budget cut, yes, but he was not prepared for being dismissed altogether. This meeting had taken on an ugly focus.

Leaving Dale University was something Professor Preston had never considered doing. He had expected to remain in his present post until retirement. As a satisfied member of the university faculty, his mind had been set on the present and not on the future.

And now this! If it wasn't budget cuts, it was one of their damned programs.

What can I say to change their decision? Professor Preston asked himself. Probably nothing. They had come to the meeting holding all the cards. He looked at each one of the directors who were waiting for an answer. Not trusting his mounting volatile emotions, Peter decided not to say anything. "No, dean, I don't have any questions at this time."

Peter tossed the red folder into his briefcase and snapped the case shut. The sound echoed ominously around the conference room. He stood up and approached the boardroom table. He shook hands with each of the directors. One murmured a "good luck" and another "I hope everything goes well" each accompanied by a feeble smile and a quick handshake.

Peter walked briskly toward the door. Just before leaving, he turned on his heel and glanced back at the pentagon group who were all watching him intently.

I'll bet their positions are secure. He walked out of the room and slammed the door.

CHAPTER 2

Alex Wiley drove his silver BMW convertible just a little too fast around the corner. One of the wheels slipped off the pavement onto the gravel shoulder causing a cloud of dust to spin up into the air. He instinctively looked in the rear-view mirror to see if another car was behind him while he righted the vehicle.

Alex could easily be described as a ball of moving energy. He was always on the go. Every day there were at least ten items on his agenda. As well as being an executive in his family's business, he sat on several committees.

Alex was twenty-seven years old. His hair was black and perfectly groomed. His eyes were the color of midnight. His body was in superb shape due to rigorous workouts. Some of his friends teasingly called him "the black sheep of the family" even though he still lived at home and was remarkably responsible.

Alex could have almost any girl he chose but, more often than not, chose to be alone. *Why?* He found it close to impossible to tolerate the flimsy conversations most females he met seemed to prefer. *How much can a person say about hair or fashion anyway?* Alex often wondered. He wanted and needed a challenge. As gorgeous as some of the women he met were, challenging they were not.

Alex was running late for a two o'clock business meeting in

Greenvale. As his car sped along the hillside road, he glanced down at the clock on the dashboard: 1:48 P.M. *Damn.* He still had another twenty minutes left to drive. If he didn't get a move on he would be late. Recently Alex noticed he was arriving late for quite a few appointments. This was unusual for him. It didn't seem to matter how well he timed things, he kept missing or being late for appointments. He promised himself he would have to cut back on his agenda or at least do some serious time management.

Even though Alex Wiley had been born wealthy he often considered it a disadvantage. People seemed to expect more from him than they did from others who were less fortunate. For instance, with this meeting he was on his way to attend, he was expected to act as chairperson and then pay for the lunch afterwards. Alex didn't consider this fair play but he felt sure if he objected it would be misunderstood.

The hill leading down into the north end of Hidden Valley was a steep descent and there were many treacherous turns in the road. Luckily Alex was familiar with every curve along the way. He had been driving these back roads since he was sixteen years old. And it was a good thing too. At the speed he was going, any other driver would have ended up in the ditch, or worse, over the cliff.

The car-phone began to ring. Alex slowed down and eased the car onto the gravel shoulder. He was not going to risk driving with one hand on this winding road. Putting the car into Park, he picked up the black console phone.

"Alex here."

"Hey Alex ... it's Ian." The voice came through intermittently.

Ian Sullivan was *Manager of Public Relations* for Wiley Industries. Among his many duties, Ian was responsible for organizing the executive meetings.

"Hi, Ian. What's up?"

"Just wanted you to know ... this afternoon's meeting's been postponed until Friday ... same time, same place. Sorry chum ... hope it doesn't put you out."

Alex's temper flared. "Terrific! I'm nearly killing myself trying to get to it. Why was it cancelled? Or should I ask?"

There was a long pause before Ian's voice came over the car-phone. "... Katherine cancelled at the last minute. She said she had some important business to attend to ... but didn't say what."

Katherine Wiley was Alex's older sister. She was *VP of Operations* in the family business. Where Alex was a reliable type, Katherine was unpredictable. She was often the cause of family problems. She and Alex rarely saw eye-to-eye. Alex had come to the conclusion Katherine wanted to run Wiley Industries all by herself. He saw her as cunning, a person who seemed to have a hidden agenda. He noticed on more than one occasion Katherine got her way by using subtle threats and occasionally even bribes. It wasn't his style of doing business.

Alex seethed. "Tell her ... next time ... to give 24-hours notice. Never mind ... *I'll* tell her myself. Thanks for calling Ian."

He placed the car-phone back into its compact holder and eased the car back out onto the road. He shook his head. This was another negative experience he had been having recently. Meetings cancelled. Being late for appointments. Getting saddled with responsibilities he shouldn't have. Nothing seemed to be working well for him anymore. Maybe it was time for a change.

CHAPTER 3

Julie Sanders dove into the clear blue water of the swimming pool at *Greenvale's Community Center.* In neat consistent strokes she began her twice-weekly routine of twenty laps. She did the breaststroke for one length of the pool and returned doing the backstroke.

At twenty-nine, Julie had a streamlined body that was as smooth as a goddess and her eyes were the color of a tropical lagoon. Her long blonde hair was tied back with a white cloth band to keep it from swirling around her face while she swam. She wore a white one-piece bathing suit cut low in the front and high on the hip.

Six months ago, Julie had been employed as a software programmer for a firm called *GameSoft.* The company specialized in making PC games for young adults. Her job was to fine-tune the programs and make them user-friendly before they were released onto the market. It had been a demanding position, one that required bouts of serious problem-solving.

Julie had been good at her job. She handled stress well. She came to work early and often left late. Her sense of team spirit was one of the reasons she was well-liked in the workplace.

But then one day, out of the blue, the firm decided to downsize. Not due to financial necessity. And not due to the corporation needing a facelift. In Julie's opinion, they did it because downsizing was the "in-thing" to do as a cost-cutting measure. Downsizing gave companies an opportunity to legitimately reorganize without the hassle of wrongful-dismissal lawsuits. It was considered a handy way to bolster profits since labor costs were the most significant of all expenses.

All the personnel at GameSoft knew their company had been successful in the few short years it had been in business. It had started off with a modest investment of two hundred thousand dollars and by the end of its first year in business was netting an annual income of more than twenty million dollars. Nevertheless, when the downsizing mood struck the executives of GameSoft, it was decided that peripheral programmers would be cut from the payroll. Julie Sanders became one of their targets.

Since her layoff, she had found it difficult to find employment opportunities in her field. Overnight it seemed her future went from a rainbow of colors to a dull gray cloud. Julie was beginning to believe the only way to save her career would be to move to a bigger city — like Bayport — some place with more hi-tech opportunities than Greenvale. But since because her family lived in the Hidden Valley district, this was a move she was only willing to make as a last resort.

Julie knew her education and skills were top-of-the-line. She was proficient at handling most programming tasks assigned to her. She rarely made errors. She was a self-taught expert in data analysis. It didn't make sense to Julie that she was suddenly no longer considered a valuable asset. *Why couldn't they have assigned me another job?* she asked herself over and over again. It was all too depressing.

As she swam, Julie decided now would be a good time to stay

fit, eat healthy, and keep mentally alert. If there was a job out there that was right for her she wanted to be ready to pounce on it. She refused to fall into the trap of mindless activities common to unemployed persons. She stayed away from window-shopping, daytime television, and gossiping on the phone with friends. No, quitting was not for her. Julie was determined to remain productive the whole day long — employed or not.

After finishing her final lap Julie climbed out of the pool. She squeezed the water out of her hair and briskly rubbed herself down with a soft white towel. She gathered up her belongings and packed them into a fishnet bag. With a bounce in her step she went to the change-room to dress.

*   *   *

A storm was gathering in floating mountains of black and purple clouds. It was moving in slowly towards the unsuspecting city of Greenvale. From the heart of the clouds came electrical charges lighting up the sky with a brilliant flash. Five seconds later, the rumbling sound of thunder echoed throughout the valley.

Rain began to fall in slanting sheets at Pineview Airport. All flights in and out were postponed.

Melanie Gold sat facing her PC in her home-office only mildly aware of the approaching storm. She was concentrating on a brochure she was designing for a new client who supported her desktop-publishing business, Gold Advertising.

Melanie specialized in doing promotions for small businesses.

Her clients appreciated quality marketing material at affordable rates. Her small company had been in operation for three years. During this time she had acquired fifty-four clients and the business was growing daily. Melanie felt confident one day Gold Advertising would become an established enterprise. Then the years she spent at college studying to be a graphic designer, as well as the small investment she began the business with, were certain to pay off in a profitable way.

Melanie was quiet and feminine. Her soft brown hair fell in a curl to her shoulders. She wore fashionable glasses to improve her vision and used only a trace of accentuating makeup. Even though she was still single, she looked forward one day to meeting someone with similar interests to hers. But, at twenty-six, what was the rush?

As she scanned the design, Melanie became more aware of the storm. *Should I shut off my computer now or can I risk it for a few more minutes?* Power surges from lightning storms can backlash through the hydro system and damage the delicate components inside a computer.

"I'd better finish this up," she decided. It was wise not to take chances when it came to power surges.

Melanie saved the file she was working on and made a back-up copy for her storage files. Meticulous work procedures were the backbone of her business. She never did anything in haste. Her work was always double-checked.

Logging off her computer, Melanie decided to flick off the power-bar switch to safely block any possible power surges.

Melanie got up and went over to the bay window. From there she could see the darkening southern sky. Melanie loved storms. Even as a child she had found them exhilarating. They made her feel energized and alive. After a few minutes she went to the kitchen to make a cup of Peppermint Tea.

CHAPTER 4

Peter lay on his plum-colored leather sofa in the living room of his ranch-style home. All the lights were off. It was starting to get dark outside.

Across his stomach slept Tangy, his short-haired Siamese cat. Tangy was purring contentedly while Peter stroked his fur.

Peter was thinking about the major decision that now lay ahead for him to make. Usually he was good at making decisions. With a little thought and some inspiration he normally could forge any path in his life. But for some reason, he found it difficult to even think about his current dilemma.

Since the fateful meeting with the university's board of directors, he had been subconsciously avoiding what had been discussed and how it affected his present life. It had all happened too fast. He couldn't seem to adjust to the sudden change that the termination had been imposed on him.

After twelve years of working for Dale University, his post was now gone. It didn't matter how noble the reason was, the truth boiled down to the fact that he was unemployed. The sting of it hurt like lemon on a paper cut.

Peter had been a dedicated professor. He had gone to work every morning bright-eyed and bushy-tailed. He had gotten along well with the other professors. He had always been cooperative with the dean and the board of trustees. If someone asked him if he thought his career was fulfilling, his immediate response would have been "Yes!"

And suddenly it was all over!

Should I start looking for another post at another university? he pondered. With all the shuffling of staff as a result of Career Focus, there might be a lot of competition. First bidders would have the advantage. If he didn't act fast, he might end up with only a junior post.

A distant part of him felt reluctant at the thought of typing a curriculum vitae. Job-hunting was something he would not have chosen to do at this stage in his life. Since he had been forced into it, he lacked the necessary get-up-and-go attitude.

"Why not use this opportunity to have a well-deserved vacation?" said a tempting voice at the back of his mind.

Hey, now that was a wonderful idea! Then he could forget about his problem and simply enjoy life for awhile. It had been years since he had the pleasure of doing exactly as he pleased.

Being a professor meant being in a constant state of either teaching or researching. There were always intellectual challenges to be faced. The amount of research a professor did alone would boggle the mind of the average citizen. Over the years, the continual mental strain became taxing. But realistically, how good would he be at being lazy? *Not so good*, Peter admitted.

Peter decided not to fight the denial any longer. The wisest thing for him to do was just let nature run its own course. He felt sure the right decision would eventually come to him. In the meantime, he would carry on as if nothing had happened. *Was there anything wrong with doing that?*

Tangy sensed his caregiver's mood improving. He stood up, stretched, jumped down onto the floor, and padded off to the kitchen to look for something to eat.

*   *   *

Peter stood in the middle of his university office surrounded by an array of empty boxes. The dreaded moment had arrived! The semester was over and now it was time to move out. The deadline for vacating his office was in two days. If he didn't get out now, he would get a call from the dean. And of course he didn't want *that* to happen.

He looked around the tidy office he had occupied for the past twelve years. Even though it was a small space, he had utilized it with maximum efficiency. Everything had its own allocated spot. Nothing was ever out of place. He kept it as neat as a pin.

The professor's degrees were framed and mounted in a semicircle on one wall. He was proud of them. They signified the years of effort he had made towards advancing his career. They also gave the office an impression of being academically official.

Next to a coat rack stood a maple bookcase. Peter was sure it had been there since the university was first built. It contained a selection of books on various topics, mostly relating to the field of technology.

As he slowly packed, Peter began to reminisce over the years he had spent teaching at Dale University. He had to admit he had loved his job. He knew he was going to miss it. Not only did Peter know his subject well, he had kept himself informed on the latest advancements in his field. For example, he could give a course itself on how to use the Internet for doing research. The Internet was one of the professor's specialties. It held challenges he enjoyed immensely.

Even though Professor Preston was not considered the most popular professor at Dale University, he was definitely one of the most respected. Anyone could go to him for an honest opinion or word-of-advice. He was steady like that.

Up until five years ago Peter had been married. During the early years of his marriage he and his wife had attended many dinner-parties, conferences, and events together. His personal life had been lively and interesting back then. Over time his wife grew restless and lost interest in the university scene. She decided to leave. Peter still missed her.

Peter removed his certificates from the wall and carefully wrapped each one in a towel before putting them in a box. Gently he packed the degrees until the box was full. He stuffed the rest of the towels in and around the empty spaces to keep the frames from shifting while in transit.

Once everything was sealed and ready to go, Peter put the boxes on a dolly he had borrowed from the maintenance department. He wheeled the dolly out to his Lexus in the parking lot. After opening the trunk of his car with his remote control, he began to store the boxes inside. He carefully positioned each one so there would be minimal movement.

After returning the dolly to the maintenance department, he surveyed the now-empty office for the last time. He felt as though he were facing the end of a chapter in his life. It had been a long and rewarding chapter. A tug of sadness welled inside him.

When he closed the office door, he noticed the plaque mounted on the outside. It read: PROF. PRESTON - COMPUTERS & TECHNOLOGY. Peter pondered on whether or not to remove the plaque to keep as a sentiment. He decided he would.

Dashing back to his car, he found a screwdriver in the glove box. Returning to his office, he carefully unscrewed the plaque from the door and slipped it into his pocket.

What does life have in store for me now? Peter wondered as he got in his car and slowly drove out the university parking lot.

CHAPTER 5

Just as the sun was beginning to rise Peter sat at his desk in his study with a lamp glowing under a green glass shade. He wore a black track suit with the zipper pulled halfway down for comfort. His sleeves were rolled up as he immersed himself with the task at hand.

Peter was sorting through a massive stack of files he had brought home from his university office. They were a testament to the amount of work he had done over the past twelve years. On the left side of his desk he placed files he wished to keep. On the right side of his desk he placed files he wished to examine more carefully. In a cardboard box on the floor beside his desk he tossed in files he planned to later shred and recycle. To his slight dismay, Peter noticed the recycle pile was becoming considerably higher than the others. *All my hard work going to waste,* he sighed, shaking his head.

Halfway through the stack, the professor came across a file he hadn't seen in years. It immediately caught his attention. On the label of the beige folder were three neat letters written in black ink: **D I M.**

Peter carefully opened the folder and withdrew a cluster of papers. Small slips of paper were clipped to a folded sheet of drafting paper at the front of the folder. Drawings and newspaper clippings were inside the folder. It was a diverse assortment of material.

Pushing his chair away from the desk, Peter began to examine the contents of the folder to refresh his memory.

DIM was the name of a *portable research computer* Professor Preston had designed seven years ago. Essentially, DIM was a computer that stored databases of articles and information that was useful in doing research. He found DIM saved him time and helped him keep his data under control. Originally he had created a test-model and used it in class. Unfortunately the test-model was stolen from his lecture room one day. Peter guessed the thief didn't realize the computer was not an ordinary PC. This event had discouraged him and caused him to temporarily abandon the project.

Peter smiled as the memories came rushing back to him. He had been so adamant about finding efficient ways to do research. He would involve anyone who was interested in lengthy discussions on the merits of using technology for the purpose of researching. Many a late night went into these lively debates.

As a professor Peter had frequently been involved in research of one kind or another. Many research tasks became tedious and frustrating because of the enormous amount of time and effort spent in manually gathering and sorting data. Sometimes a mountain of information had to be sifted through before even a handful of suitable material was amassed. The need for a quicker method of finding things led him to the idea of designing a portable research computer.

Professor Preston knew research computers were common in places like labs and scientific research centers. But these machines were huge and often filled an entire room. His DIM model could easily sit on top of a desk, making it a more convenient solution.

All the preliminary work was done for the design of DIM and

the notes and drawings neatly placed in this folder. Unfortunately, the project had been filed away for "future reference" like so many other projects Professor Preston had done over the years. Such were the demands of a university professor.

Peter could feel the file humming in his hands as though it were still alive with a viable idea.

He began to wonder if there could be a market for DIM since nobody could go out and buy a research computer in a store. They were not commercially available. Peter thought they should be. He could think of many instances where a research computer might be handy to have both in business and education.

Could a commercial product of DIM be made? Peter wondered. *And if it could, would it be marketable?*

These were the questions Professor Preston began asking himself while he studied the designs of his invention. The answer to the first question was easy: *Yes! It would be easy to manufacture the DIM model.* But the answer to the second question was not so easy. He would need to do a market study to determine whether or not DIM would be profitable as a commercial product.

Professor Preston was aware that no product could survive on the market unless it had a lot of satisfied customers. For it to be a success the DIM computer would have to be popular with specialized groups, like teachers and writers, as well as the general public.

During his career Peter had watched many good ideas become isolated within a particular professional field. He witnessed hours of work go into the writing of books that were eventually read only by a handful of other professionals. *What a waste!* Peter would think as he witnessed this happening. No ordinary citizen ever got to read this knowledge or utilize some of their extraordinary secrets. Just like UFO findings were hidden away from the public by the government, so were many intellectual concepts.

Peter didn't want his DIM invention to become a "closet" product. He wanted it to be available for everyone to use.

How can I interest an ordinary person into buying a research computer? This was going to be a challenge. Thinking about it all afternoon an idea suddenly came to him. He could promote the uses of the DIM computer when he marketed the product. If people knew how to use the computer in different ways they were more likely to give it a try.

Public demonstrations could then be done to teach people how to use their DIM computer. Between these demos and the Uses Manual his customers would soon catch on.

Peter spent hours thinking up scenarios that a DIM computer could be used in. He wrote down each scenario on its own separate sheet of paper. By the evening he had a folder full of possibilities:

> A travel agent could use DIM to help find their clients the perfect accommodations.

> A student could use DIM to do research for a school project.

> A video storeowner could use DIM for helping customers find movies starring a particular actor or actress.

> A physician could use DIM to help diagnose a patient with an unknown illness.

Since his post was terminated at Dale University, Peter was facing a wall of time. His planner had gone from full to empty in a few short weeks. Where in the past he had no time to take on a venture such as this one, now he had all the time in the world.

Could I start a company and sell my DIM computers? Peter considered this as a possible career option.

Obtaining the necessary finances to start a new business was not likely to be an obstacle for him. Over the years he had collected quite a nest-egg for himself. Since he had no children, his money was available to do with as he pleased. He owned his own home which was also an asset. His pension could be withdrawn early. There was even money left over from an inheritance he had received from his late father, Archie Preston. He also owned several hundred stocks in various technology businesses. All he had to do was say the word "sell" to his broker and these investments could be turned into liquid cash. All in all Peter estimated he had access to $1.3 million dollars with another $200,000 for emergency use.

Would this be enough money to start a hi-tech company if I am careful and clever how I do it?

With his Ph.D. in Computer Science and twelve years teaching experience, Peter knew his knowledge could become the backbone in the business. And what he didn't know he would learn.

But do I have the nerve?

The corporate world was unpredictable compared to the safe sanctuary of the educational world. It only took one bad decision and an entrepreneur could lose his shirt overnight. There were more cases of riches-to-rags than there were rags-to-riches. The stress of running a business alone could be horrendous. Many business people died young from heart failure directly due to stress.

Will I buckle under this pressure?

Professor Preston felt sure he wouldn't. Stress was something he actually thrived on. It stimulated him. If he could control a class full of rowdy first-year students he felt sure he could easily manage a group of well-trained personnel. Even the odd unhappy customer wasn't likely to shake Peter's confidence.

Becoming rich wasn't important to Peter. He was already modestly well off. For many years he had enjoyed a prosperous lifestyle. It wasn't the thought of getting rich that inspired him; it was the thought of contributing something worthwhile to the world of technology.

He began to feel certain this was the path he was meant to take. Maybe it was even the reason why he was so reluctant to rush out and apply for a post at another university. Peter decided then and there he would start a company to sell a commercial version of his DIM portable research computer.

*　　*　　*

The next few days were a bustle of activity at the professor's home. Peter worked every day on the DIM project sometimes until well passed midnight. He set up a file cabinet in his study specifically for the project. He redid the invention sketches neatly on sheets of tracing paper. He re-typed his notes on his laptop computer and printed fresh copies. He placed the notes inside labeled folders and stored them in the file cabinet.

Peter developed a basic budget for the project. Not knowing what the real costs would be, he estimated them. Beside the items that needed further inquiry he put question marks. He intended to be frugal when it came to starting the company.

Peter became more enthusiastic each time he worked on the DIM project. It unleashed a hidden sense of adventure in him he never realized he had. In all his life Peter had never done anything as exciting before. Most of his life had been an ongoing exercise in conservatism. Going from a professor to an entrepreneur was like transforming from a caterpillar to a butterfly. Soon he would be testing his new wings.

CHAPTER 6

Alex was a computer engineer who had never actually used his skills. Like many offspring of wealthy families, he had attended university because it was expected of him. But when it came time to graduate he was encouraged to pursue other ventures. For the sake of the family business he took up these ventures silently, without complaint, and reluctantly stored his university textbooks away in the attic of his parent's home.

Initially Alex didn't object. He would say to himself, *there is always tomorrow.* But now, ten years later, tomorrow had never come for him, at least not as far as a computer-based career was concerned anyway.

Recently he found himself thinking about his long-lost degree. *What was the point in getting it?* A sense of nostalgia grew in him every time he saw a computer. He thought of his abandoned career as something that was floating around in cyberspace, not doing any good for anyone.

A mild depression settled over Alex as he thought of the deals and sacrifices he was forced to make for the sake of the family business. They seemed to getting deeper, darker, and more dishonest. How far was a person supposed to go to make an already wealthy family even richer? *Enough is enough!* Alex decided one day.

Late one night, when nobody else was home, Alex slipped up into the attic of the Wiley mansion home. The room had slanted ceilings and two small porthole windows at either end. An inch of dust covered over everything. *When was the last time anybody was up here?* Alex wondered as he began poking through a haphazard collection of storage boxes.

He searched through boxes and trunks without finding anything. Then, just as he was about to give up, he discovered his university textbooks tucked away in a blue trunk with gold clasps in the farthest corner of the attic. It was as though someone were deliberately trying to hide them. Alex dragged the trunk over to one of the windows. By the light of the full moon, in the midst of cobwebs and dust, he browsed through the pages of his forgotten textbooks.

Alex remembered how fascinated he had once been with computers. He once felt technology was a part of him — that he himself was a hi-tech being in human form. For several years he and his geek colleagues at Bayport University had obsessed over bits, bytes, and motherboards. There was nothing they couldn't put together with a collection of inner workings of computer hardware. Alex's genius allowed him to be a member of the secret club of computer assemblers.

He yearned for those days again. Nothing in his present life even remotely gave him the thrill that codes and chips and computers once did. He could tell the knowledge was still there at the back of his mind. It just needed to be re-connected to his brain again.

The feeling of frustration that had plagued Alex for the past few weeks began to dissipate. A burden lifted off his shoulders making him feel light-headed. The cloud of uncertainty dispersed, revealing clear skies once more. He was reunited with his destiny!

Alex gathered up his textbooks and put them in brown-paper shopping bags he found scattered nearby on the floor. He dusted the cobwebs off his jeans and went back down to his private suite of rooms in the west wing.

CHAPTER 7

After a summer of heat-waves and thunderstorms cooler air moved into Hidden Valley adding a feeling of relief. Summer had ended and fall was about to begin.

A blue heron with a two-foot wingspan flew above the flat plane of ground with its wings swooshing through the air. Hidden Valley was a breeding spot for many exotic birds including herons, storks, and egrets. The area had recently been declared a bird sanctuary and now maintained strict environmental regulations. Any one caught disturbing the nests of these protected birds would find themselves paying stiff fines.

That morning Peter was preparing for a trip to the country. He wanted to find a suitable building he could use as a factory to manufacture the DIM computers. It had to be someplace that could not be easily found. It was his intention to keep everything relating to his new company a secret for as long as possible. *Why?* For one important reason.

Professor Preston and the students in one of his courses did a study of w*hat happens to small technology companies after they became successful?* The class observed that a noticeable number of new hi-tech firms became the targets of a corporate merger of some kind. Some of these mergers were friendly while others were not so friendly. Most were done in the guise of *merging intelligence to create better technology.* The class noted, however, better technology did not necessarily emerge after these acquisitions took place. In fact, in some cases the larger of the two companies absorbed the worth of the target company and what was left over was simply tossed out. This often included the smaller company's name, product, and its employees.

Peter surmised the reason why these mergers happened was partly the fault of the media. When grand-scale publicity was done, the media inadvertently exposed details about uprising firms to the executives of mega corporations. Articles published by the media allowed executives to discover who the owners were, where their offices were located, and any pertinent statistical data about the upstart firm. The sharp-minded CEO's would then target the fledgling firm with a merger prospect. Since new company owners were flattered by the attention, they soon gave in to the demands.

Peter concluded if media publicity had been subdued then fewer executives would find about these overnight sensations. Unfortunately, he and the class realized this might include the customers too.

Peter didn't want his new company, DIM Inc., to become a victim of a forced merger, if he could help it. But he wasn't sure how to go about preventing this from happening. As a professor he wasn't knowledgeable in the ways of business. He wondered, for example, how a magnate of a conglomerate could get a small business owner to hand over the keys to his thriving new company. It couldn't be for money since most of these new firms were rich in their own right. *Was it by threat?*

Peter was afraid of finding out. So he created a strategy plan to guard his new company from a possible takeover. There were two parts to his plan. First he planned to hide the factory and keep its location a secret. He would tell only those who needed to know where it was and request this information be kept confidential. Second he would forego doing publicity interviews at least until the company was well established. He would advertise the product, of course, and customer service would be made available but information relating to the owner, the factory's location, and financial data would be kept top secret.

Peter didn't think a customer needed to see a picture of him in a high-profile magazine to feel confident about making a purchase. The product should sell itself.

He made a commitment to DIM Inc. through his strategy plan. If he was going to go to the trouble of setting up a new business, and making it a success, then he was going to keep it — for as long as possible.

Peter's plan was to drive up and down the concession roads outside of Greenvale looking for a hideaway place for DIM's factory. It had to be away from the industrial zone where local companies usually kept their factories down in the southwest region of Greenvale. Peter went east instead.

He packed a notepad and a pen, a digital camera, a flashlight, a pair of binoculars, and a small lunch. He put these items into a blue canvas duffel bag and stored it in the back seat of his car. Climbing into the driver's seat, he set out to find DIM a home.

*   *   *

It was 10:05 in the morning as Peter drove leisurely along Concession Road #1 five miles east of Greenvale. The heat from the sun had dissolved the morning mist. Splashes of gold and crimson illuminated the surrounding forest as the fall leaves had begun to change color. The sky was blue and the air was crisp and fresh.

Easy-listening music played quietly on the car stereo. Sipping coffee from the thermos, Peter listened to the music while he drove up and down the county roads scanning for suitable buildings. He excluded barns because they were generally not winterized or sturdy enough.

Around one o'clock in the afternoon Peter decided to stop, stretch his legs, and have a bite of lunch. He had been driving steadily for three hours. Peter parked the Lexus at the entrance of a sandy pathway. It couldn't properly be called a road although it may have once been one. There were shaggy raspberry bushes growing wild on either side of the tracks. In the center of the path tall clumps of barley grass had grown to a height of two feet.

Peter took the canvas duffel bag out from the back seat of his car and slung it over his shoulder. He plucked a blade of grass and popped it into the corner of his mouth. Strolling along the sandy path, he suddenly felt good to be alive. There were no worries out here in the woods. Time seemed to stand still. A feeling of peacefulness settled over him.

One hundred yards down the path he came to a wooden bridge over a fast-running river. Leaning against the railing, Peter looked down into the churning waters. He could tell the water was cold just by the look of it.

Peter breathed in the oxygen-laden air while he continued walking. Soon he came to a clearing. A large boulder made of gray granite stone etched with red streaks sat to the left. Peter mildly wondered how it got there. He plopped his duffel bag down on top of the rock and stretched his arms.

"What a great day!" he said out loud.

As he stood gazing around the clearing, Peter caught sight of something brown beyond a line of evergreen trees. Keen to find out what it was, he took the binoculars out of his duffel bag and peered through the lenses. He could definitely see a building, about two stories high, made of dark brown bricks and thick wooden beams.

I wonder what that building is. His curiosity was piqued.

Peter decided to investigate it. Picking up the duffel bag, he walked across the clearing towards the row of white pine trees. When he got to the trees, he could clearly see that it was indeed a building. It was at least a hundred years old, he surmised. It had been built on a flat plane of land. There were trees on both sides of the building, a grassy area in the front and what looked like an open meadow at the back. A faded sign mounted on the front of the building said: The **Snap Glue Company**. Peter realized the building must have once been a glue factory. *What luck!*

He ventured closer to the building being careful to watch out for boards with nails sticking out of them, broken glass, and snakes lurking in the grass. It would be easy to step on something without seeing it first, he realized, as he waded through the knee-high grass.

The front door was locked with a huge rusty padlock. Peter pulled on the lock but it wouldn't budge. It looked like it had been there for several decades.

Peter dropped his duffel bag on the ground and tested a nearby window instead. He was able to unlatch the window by reaching his had through a broken pane of glass. The enormous window swung open to the inside. Bits of paint and plaster rained down over Peter's head. He brushed off the crumbs with both his hands. Using a long stick he found on the ground nearby, Peter propped the window open.

He threw the duffel bag in first. Jumping through the open window, Peter landed with a thud on the floor inside. The sound echoed throughout the empty building. A few startled bats flew across a dark area of the ceiling. Peter's heart-rate began to accelerate.

He gazed in awe around the immense empty space. The ceiling had to be at least one hundred feet high. Peter estimated the space he was standing in to be at least five thousand square feet.

Several pieces of abandoned machinery lay scattered on the floor. They must once have been used when the glue factory was in operation. Walking carefully around the debris, Peter began to explore the building. He soon discovered there were actually two areas of almost equal size. One area was perpendicular to the other making the building L-shaped.

As he walked, he took pictures with his camera of the floor, ceiling, windows, doors, and a staircase. He climbed the rickety stairs and discovered a vacant loft. Peter sat down on the top step. From this vantage point he could see the entire expanse of the building below.

What a fantastic place!

Peter began to envision how the building could be transformed into a factory for assembling the DIM computers. The area directly below him would be ideal for design and administration tasks. The area in the back of the building would be ideal for assembling and storing the final product. There were even a couple of storage rooms that would be handy for inventory and supplies.

He climbed down the stairs and headed towards the back area. A monstrous set of double-doors was held closed by a lever bar. Peering through a nearby window Peter could see a ramp outside. *Perfect for shipping and receiving,* he thought.

Peter went back outside through the window and walked around the circumference of the building. He imagined once a better road was laid along the sandy track, the clearing area would be ideal for a staff parking lot. He would leave most of the trees standing because they helped shield the building as a hideaway.

Peter considered what renovations would need to be done to the building. He jotted some ideas down on the notepad: patching floors, new windows, insulation, sand-blast bricks, and industrial ceiling fans.

In terms of starting his new company, Peter thought the property was perfect. Because of its somewhat dilapidated condition, he was sure he could buy it for a reasonable price. It was certainly remote enough. If he hadn't stumbled across it, he would never have found it otherwise.

Peter glanced around for fences trying to get an idea of how large the property was. The land went as far as the eye could see to the north. But to the south there was a white board fence separating the property from a farm next door.

After he finished making his notes, Peter sat down on the granite boulder and leisurely ate his lunch of sockeye-salmon sandwiches, a pear, and a bottle of spring water.

Peter strolled back to the Lexus. Just before leaving he wrote down the exact location of the building and programmed his GPS navigation system. A few minutes later he was heading home to Greenvale.

CHAPTER 8

"How may I help you?" The young clerk in the Planner's Office at City Hall leaned against the other side of the counter and smiled at Professor Preston. She was in her early twenties and fully aware of her attractive appearance. Outfitted in a snug cherry-colored suit and a cream silk blouse, she played with the end of a long gold chain.

The professor had spent the better part of his teaching years warding off the advances of provocative female students but, to this day, was still not comfortable handling these awkward moments. In a deep voice he replied, "I want to find out who the owner is of a property located outside the city limits. Here are the coordinates."

Peter pushed a slip of paper across the counter towards the clerk. She picked it up slowly never once taking her eyes off his face and then glanced quickly over the note.

The Snap Glue Company, Concession Road # 5, just north of Airport Road.

"May I ask the reason for this request?" The clerk raised one eyebrow.

The professor answered, "Of course," moving up and down on his heels. "I am considering buying this property. It isn't listed for sale, so I need to speak with the present owner."

"I suppose that would be OK then. If you would like to take a seat over there..." She pointed to a chair next to a water cooler. "I'll see what I can find out ... and be right back." And as if he might suddenly disappear she fixed him a mesmerizing gaze before turning to go.

Peter went and sat down on the chair. While he waited he thought about his decision to buy the old factory building. It seemed the right thing to do partly because there was something special about the way he had found it and partly because it would be ideal for his purposes. In a mysterious sort of way he had been drawn to the very place the building was located. *Was that a coincidence?* Peter wasn't superstitious but this made for an exceptional case. It only seemed natural to follow up on it.

Five minutes later the clerk returned to the counter with a green folder in her hands. She placed it on the countertop and gave Peter a nod to indicate she was ready.

The professor stood up and approached the counter. "Did you find anything out?" he asked enthusiastically.

"Yes. I believe so," countermanded the clerk. She opened the folder, withdrew the contents, and placed them on top of the counter. "The present owner of property is ... Emily Fairbanks. Her address is here in Greenvale ... but I think it would be better if you called her first."

She wrote a phone number on the back of the slip of paper the professor had given her and handed it to him. "It's always a good idea to be discreet when it comes to legal matters. Is there anything else I can help you with?" There was that soft subtle smile again.

Peter decided he'd better leave now or he'd end up with two

phone numbers instead of one. Beaming a smile at the clerk, he replied, "No, but thanks for your help. I really appreciate it."

*   *   *

At seven o'clock in the evening, Peter arrived at the home of Emily Fairbanks on Stratton Street. He rang the doorbell. A few minutes later a woman in her late seventies opened the beveled-glass door and welcomed her visitor. "Good evening. You must be Peter Preston. Won't you come in?"

Peter shook Emily's delicate hand and stepped into the hallway. He took off his coat and hung it up on a brass coat-tree next to a gold-framed mirror. Peter quickly glanced in the mirror to see if his hair was in order before heading down the hall.

Emily invited him into the living room where a fire was burning brightly in a mosaic stone fireplace. Two colorful Tiffany lamps on either side of the fireplace added to the room's cozy ambience.

Peter went over to the fire rubbing his hands briskly together. "You have a lovely home, Mrs. Fairbanks," he complimented his hostess.

"Thank you ... and please call me Emily." She stood graciously in the center of the room. "Would you like a cup of tea? I've just made some."

"Yes, that would be nice." Peter chose a tapestry-covered armchair close to the fire and sat down.

Emily returned a few minutes later carrying a tray with two

44

mugs of hot tea and two slices of homemade chocolate cake. She set the tray down on a wooden coffee table and began to serve her guest. While they enjoyed their refreshments, they chatted about how hot the summer had been.

Twenty minutes later, Peter set his mug down on a paper napkin and linked his fingers together. "As I said briefly on the phone this afternoon, Emily, I would like to make an offer to purchase the property where the former Snap Glue company was located. I understand from the Planner's Office at City Hall that you are the present owner. Is there any chance you might consider selling it to me?"

Emily began to laugh light-heartedly. "That old place! I'd almost forgotten about it. My great-grandfather built it, you know. It has been a legacy in our family for more than one hundred years. I'm afraid it has been dreadfully neglected. I'm not really sure I should sell it … considering the condition it is in … " her voiced trailed off.

Peter took advantage of the pause in her soliloquy to say, "The condition of the building is OK by me since I plan to do my own renovations. As a matter-of-fact I intend to set up a factory of my own. The building would be ideal for my purposes. It would allow me to start my company off economically. If the price isn't too high, I would be willing to purchase the building and whatever land comes with it."

He smiled at his hostess.

Emily leaned closer and whispered to the professor as though she were divulging a great secret to him. "Did you know there are *fifty* acres of land belonging to that property?"

"No, I hadn't realized that." Peter was pleased with this bonus bit of information. Owning a sizable piece of land would allow for expansion if his company became successful. "I have done a casual survey of the property and am prepared to offer you $350,000 ... for the building and the property."

Emily's eyes lit up momentarily. "That is a very generous offer, Mr. Preston. It is of no use to me obviously. But it would be nice to see it made useful again."

Peter agreed with her. "Yes, it's a great spot. If I bought it I would renovate the building up to standard."

Emily filled Peter in with details about the origins of the factory. She explained how her great-grand-father had once run a successful business there. "Why don't you let me think about your offer for a couple of days, Peter. You can call me on Friday morning ... say ten o'clock. I'll have an answer by then."

"Fair enough, Emily."

Later when Peter stepped out into the cool evening air he had a momentary feeling of elation.

*   *   *

Two weeks later Peter Preston officially became the owner of Lot 66 on Concession Road #5. A survey revealed there were 55.6 acres of land on the property and there were no liens against it. The sale went through without a hitch.

Emily thanked Peter for his cheque in the amount of $350,000 when they met at her solicitor's office in downtown Greenvale.

"I hope your company goes well, Peter."

"Thank you, Emily. I hope so too," said Peter in a positive tone.

He offered to give her a ride back to her house but she politely declined saying she had some errands to run first. They said good-bye and each went their own separate way.

CHAPTER 9

Renovations to the old factory building began in the spring of the following year. As Emily put it, "It's about time something was done to the place!" The building had been sitting idle for close to forty years. The swath of two-foot grass surrounding the property was a testament to its neglect.

A modest renovation plan was drawn up and a local contractor from Greenvale hired to do the work. The basic plan was to keep the original structure intact and use whatever was already there to its best advantage. The renovation costs were estimated in the $70,000 range give or take a few thousand dollars. The deadline for completion was set for May 15th.

Peter Preston stood in the clearing area with a clipboard in hand watching the men at work. They were in the process of taking down the old sign mounted over the front door. A new sign would soon take its place saying: RESEARCH TECHNOLOGY EQUIPMENT.

Peter felt a small surge of pride as he surveyed the improvements that had been done to the building so far. All the windows had been replaced with new ones now gleaming in the morning sun. Each window could be opened to allow fresh air inside the factory. This was necessary for improving air circulation during the hot summer months.

The outside surface of the bricks had been sand-blasted and was now a light shade of brown. The window frames, doors, and trim had all been painted a teal color. Peter thought the blue-green shade did a lot to cheer up the look of the old building since the former color had been railway-brown.

The sandy pathway leading in from the concession road had been widened and covered over with a layer of smooth pebbles making it a proper driveway that opened to a sand-packed parking lot where Peter was now standing. At least fifty cars could be parked in the lot.

Peter greeted the workmen as he went inside the building. Immediately the scent of newly-cut plywood greeted him. He walked over to a makeshift desk on a workhorse where the renovation plans were laid out. Placing his clipboard on one end of the desk, Peter picked up his coffee mug and began to browse around the building.

The entire expanse of the factory had been cleared out. The abandoned pieces of machinery had been taken away to a scrap-metal depot for recycling. Thankfully the floor was still in excellent shape in most places. It was an oak floor and, true to its form, had endured throughout the years. Oak is one of the hardest woods in the forest. The only portions of the floor that needed to be replaced were underneath the windows and in front of the doors where a little rain had seeped through and softened these spots.

Suspended from the ceiling were ten new industrial fans with six-foot gray blades gracefully spinning at a low speed. Peter decided fans would be a better investment than air-conditioning since the factory was located near a river. Air conditioning was expensive and

Peter didn't want to waste any investment money.

A sunny lunchroom was set up at the south end of the assembly area for personnel use. New tables and chairs were positioned across the length of the room. A water cooler had been installed in a corner of the lunchroom as well as a coin-operated beverage machine. Two new washrooms were built adjacent to the lunchroom.

The walls in the factory had been painted a light shade of gray, a color in keeping with the industrial theme. The delivery doors had been replaced by a roll-up metal door which could be operated via remote-control from both inside and outside the building. Leading down from the delivery door was a wooden ramp intended for shipping and receiving. The ramp needed to be repaired and two of the workers were discussing the best way to do this when Peter came sauntering by.

"How's it going, fellas?" Peter said as he jumped down onto the ground. "Any problems?"

One of the workers lifted his cap off his head and brushed away a sheath of sweat with his sleeve. "We were just discussing how wide this ramp should be. We think maybe it should jut out about three feet before making the decline. That way boxes can be brought out onto the ledge first before being loaded onto a delivery truck. You see, sir, some trucks have their own forklifts. If there's a ledge they can just pull the boxes right off the platform and into the truck. It would make things go a lot easier."

"Sounds like a *great* idea to me. Go ahead and do it that way." Peter gave the worker a pat on the back and strode inside the factory.

He could feel a sense of dignity in the atmosphere now, as well as a hint of suspense, as though something exciting were about to happen here. He knew factories were capable of generating enormous amounts of energy. They were like invisible turbines of power. Controlled by the systems that ran the business, and fueled by the activities of the workers, the turbines could transform this power into wheels of fortune. He felt the thrill of the business's future potential beginning to happen.

Peter walked back to the administrative area and climbed the new four-foot wide staircase leading to the newly renovated loft. He wore a pair of khaki pants with numerous pockets on the sides of each leg. These pockets were filled with items like keys, pencils, notepad, and a penlight for seeing in the dark. In his shirt pocket he kept his cell-phone. He used it mainly for discussing plans with the contractor.

The loft had been made into an open-concept apartment. Peter planned to live her for the next few months. He had put his house in Greenvale up for sale. It was an interim step though. Living in the factory would be cheaper and handy for getting to and from work. He knew he could adjust to the change knowing a better life-style lay ahead.

There were four sections to the efficiency unit: one area for living, one for sleeping, one for bathing, and the fourth area for cooking and dining. Everything in the loft was painted white. The floors were covered with a plush emerald-green carpet. The wooden beams had been sanded and varnished. A fan above the main living area kept the air circulating.

On the south wall of the loft was a glass enclosure jutting out of the side of the building like a giant diamond. Peter was an amateur astronomer and planned to set up a miniature observatory in this area. Over the years Peter had accumulated an elaborate collection of astronomy equipment. As an active member of the *Hidden Valley Astronomy Club* he pursued this hobby with zeal.

The bedroom in the loft had a bubble skylight in the ceiling directly over the place where Peter's king-size bed would be placed. He wanted to be able to look at the stars at night. Being several miles out in the country meant the sky was darker than it was in the city making more stars visible to the naked eye. Light was now pouring through the skylight like honey over the floor.

Leading off the bedroom was a compact bathroom. The tiles on the floor and around the sink were dark green. There was a toilet, a vanity, and a small shelf for personal items. A steam shower had been installed in one corner. This new spa equipment was designed to help relieve stress built up during a hard day of working. Peter was looking forward to trying it out.

Tucked away in a nook was a tiny kitchen containing most of the necessary conveniences for modest cooking. It resembled the galley of a yacht. There was a mini fridge, a microwave, a small electric stove, and a porcelain sink for washing up. The cupboard space was a long shelf above the sink.

Peter sat on the top step of the staircase sipping his coffee and surveying the expanse of the factory below. It was a superb view. It enjoyed looking down at the buzz of activity below him.

He knew he was crossing a threshold into a new life, one where he was entirely the master of his own destiny. Peter considered himself an inventor now as well as an entrepreneur. He had advanced himself willingly into this illustrious career. There was no turning back. The only path was forward now — win or lose — and he promised himself he would stay on this course no matter what the future held.

His conservative ways were falling away from him like a layer of dead skin. Underneath was something more vibrant. He liked the energy it inspired in him. It made him feel years younger and full of life. Now it was *his* turn to take the world by a storm.

Peter was surprised at how quickly he gotten over his dilemma with losing his job. It was only a year ago since his post at Dale University had been terminated. Yet here he was about to launch a new business. There was nothing depressing about his situation now.

The men were preparing to leave for the day after completing another binge of renovations. "See you tomorrow Mr. Preston," one of the workers called up to Peter.

"You bet!" he replied with a wave of his hand.

CHAPTER 10

On May 1st the renovations to the factory were completed and done to Peter's satisfaction. He paid the contractor the remaining money due and thanked him for a job well done.

Peter and his cat Tangy moved into the loft apartment on the following Saturday afternoon. With the help of a former neighbor, he loaded up his belongings into a rent-a-truck and headed for the country. It took Peter the better part of the day to get everything unpacked and tucked away in his new living quarters.

He organized the loft to be similar to an efficiency unit at a resort. It included all the necessities for everyday living but not much else. Unneeded items were placed in one of the storage rooms at the back of the factory warehouse. Peter put a padlock on the door to keep things safe from intruders.

Later that evening Peter sat on his plum-colored sofa facing the gas-lit fireplace. Even though winter was over there was still enough of a chill in the air to warrant a fire. He sipped a cup of Belgian hot chocolate and was thinking of how peaceful it was in the country. Since the building was situated a good distance from the concession road there were no sounds of traffic. The only sounds came from nature or whatever was going on inside the building.

*　　*　　*

Around four o'clock in the morning Peter woke up suddenly in bed in a dredge of sweat. It felt as though the magic lights had been turned off and everything returned back to the way it used to be. Peter could feel a creeping fear seep into him.

After a moment of reflection he realized what the problem was. Since embarking on this new DIM project Peter had not thought much about the other side of his current situation. He had been too focused on the imagined future and all the wonderful things yet to come. Because of his zealousness he had neglected to see his life the way it really was. The truth boiled down to a few simple facts: his career was at a standstill; he was officially ranked as unemployed; his house in town was up for sale; none of his friends knew where he was; and now here he was living alone out in the middle of nowhere in the eerie confines of a hundred-year-old building. On top of this he had invested a considerable sum of money into a new business venture with no way of knowing whether the business would succeed or fail. If this venture failed, as many new businesses often did, Peter would be in trouble.

He could hide from these facts no longer.

As this awareness penetrated the euphoric sphere that had been surrounding him, Peter became chilled at the thought of possible failure.

Will I lose everything if my company fails?

Before panic could overcome him Peter sat up in bed and got control over himself. "I refuse to think like this," he said out loud. He knew his DIM invention was worth this effort. He fully intended to find out if a successful business could be made selling the research computers on the market. He believed in DIM. In fact, he believed in DIM more than he did in many of the things he had taught in his courses at the university.

Taking a few deep breaths he carefully pushed away the doubt and negative vibes.

As if sensing Peter's distress, Tangy suddenly appeared out from nowhere. Jumping up onto the bed the cat began purring and rubbing himself up against the professor. "Thanks, Tangy," murmured Peter. "What would I ever do without you?" He petted Tangy for a few minutes before drifting back to sleep.

CHAPTER 11

Peter woke up feeling refreshed and ready to begin a new day. When he remembered the scary moment he had in the middle of the night he was thankful it was over. He realized no business owner could guarantee the success of his or her company. All they could do was try. If he were fortunate, the company would be successful and make a lot of money. If he was not so lucky, the company would break even and his investment would be returned to him. The worst thing that could happen would be for him to go back to teaching at another university. *Was that so bad?*

Part of the effort in starting a new company was in the determination to succeed. Peter could feel a stronger resolution growing inside him. The challenge of the business had become a driving force in his life. Now he had to see it through! It would take more than a moment of doubt to make him quit. After making a cup of cappuccino in the tiny kitchenette, Peter went over to the observatory and began to plan his day.

* * *

The Lexus was warmed up for a day of errands in the city. As Peter turned left onto the concession road he glanced at the new sign mounted at the entranceway. It said simply: R.T.E. - SHIPPING & RECEIVING AT REAR with an arrow pointing in the direction of the lane way. This sign was one of several that had recently been erected in strategic spots between Greenvale and the factory. They were intended to assist visitors and delivery persons in finding the site.

Peter enjoyed the five-mile drive into Greenvale. He now made the trip two or three times a week. It had become one of the most relaxing times in his busy life. Along the road were evergreens of every kind: blue spruce, red spruce, white pine, cedar, as well as many types of deciduous trees. The scent of pine that filled the air was heady and invigorating. Occasionally a cottontail rabbit or deer would bound across the road and disappear in the bush on the other side. Luckily the roads were usually clear so Peter had no trouble getting to where he wanted to go.

When he arrived in Greenvale he parked the Lexus at the corner of Brook and Heron Streets. It was the location of a *shared executive services* business where Peter had rented an office on the main floor. His was one of ten offices using the same general facilities.

Room #103 was a sunlit office that contained a desk, a bookshelf, a telephone, and several comfortable chairs. An equipment room down the hall allowed Peter use of the fax machine, photocopier, scanner, and other equipment. He was also permitted to book the conference room for meetings. Peter found this arrangement handy as a temporary way to do in-town business.

He had rented the shared office space for three months. He intended to use it primarily for doing interviews to hire personnel to work in his new company. Once this was accomplished he planned to move into his office at the factory.

Peter's main task today was reviewing a stack of résumés that had come in as a result of an ad placed in the *Greenvale Times* and on several employment websites on the Internet.

Over the years Peter had become an organizational wizard. He could achieve large feats of work in a short space of time simply by the way he planned things. By three o'clock that afternoon he had a list of persons whom he wished to interview, questions he planned to ask, and an interview timetable. His plan was to hire three people for his design team: a graphic designer, a software programmer, and a computer hardware specialist. He also planned to hire a marketing manager to run a small office out of Bayport. This second location would be used for promoting the company and for processing direct sales.

In addition to these key personnel, Peter planned to hire a part-time bookkeeper, an office assistant, and twelve initial factory workers. As the company progressed more personnel would be added to the task force.

Peter knew it wasn't enough to hire qualified persons to do their job. He wanted competent personnel who got along well together. He knew from past experience that a harmonious work environment inspired greater productivity. In turn, this would bring in more revenue to the company.

Once Peter was finished, he tidied the office, locked the door, and departed the building.

* * *

Peter walked to the downtown core of Greenvale a few blocks away. He went to a store called *Gourmet Cuisine* to buy some supplies for a celebration dinner to mark the beginning of his new career.

Peter had considered asking a few friends to join him but changed his mind since he had already told most of them he would be away for a few months. Besides, he rationalized if he were to invite anyone over to the factory it would mean a lot of explaining and he wasn't prepared to do that just yet. So he decided this time he'd celebrate alone.

At the checkout counter the clerk recognized Peter and said teasingly, "Getting ready for a big date?" This was one of their usual banters they exchanged when he came to shop at the store. "Not this time, Rosemary. It's just me and the cat, I'm afraid." Rosemary sighed and shook her head as if to say it was shame that a good-looking eligible bachelor should have to eat alone.

Whistling softly to himself Peter took his bundle and left the store. Soon he was heading back to the country.

*　　*　　*

Peter began his preparations for the celebration dinner early Sunday afternoon. He wore a pinstriped chef's apron he had once bought on a vacation. He put a *Kenny G* CD on his stereo system to get him in the mood for an afternoon of creative cooking. He opened a cold bottle of white chardonnay wine to sip while he worked. There was no hurrying the preparation of a fine dinner.

Few men are great chefs. Peter was one of these rare gems. He could prepare a gourmet dinner that was not only delicious but healthy too. He used these occasions as a chance to explore his imaginative side.

The menu for his celebration dinner tonight included: a shrimp, sprouts, and avocado salad with a creamy ranch dressing, green beans sautéed in a hot ginger sauce, baked potatoes with sour cream and chives, and a whole rainbow trout stuffed with savory herbs and butter. For dessert Peter made a raspberry pie that would later be topped with whipped cream and grated nutmeg. After dinner Peter planned to concoct his own version of a "pirate" rum coffee.

Around six-thirty in the evening Peter set a place for himself at the dining room table in the loft alcove. He laid out the hand-painted dishes and nickel-plated silverware. He lit a pair of tall indigo candles in the center of the table.

Peter served himself a healthy portion of each dish and sat down to eat. Immediately his appetite sprang to life. He ate his meal leisurely while listening to the music in the background. It was a pleasant interlude.

When he was through he put a few morsels of trout in Tangy's food dish. Wherever he was he would be around later to enjoy it.

Peter cleared away the dishes and put them to soak in the porcelain sink. He made his specialty coffee and settled down on the sofa to watch a DVD he had bought in Greenvale; it was a new science-fiction release called *MoonLife*. The movie held him captivated from beginning to end.

CHAPTER 12

Sunday May 16, 9:30 p.m.

As Alex drove slowly along the pebbled driveway he began to experience a sense of déjà vu. *Have I been here before?* It must have been during his childhood days because he knew it had not been recently.

He drove slowly over a wooden bridge until he came to a clearing. There were no other cars in the lot. He parked his BMW close to the front of the building. When Alex got out of his car he noticed the sign mounted on the front of the old edifice: RESEARCH TECHNOLOGY EQUIPMENT.

A company? Why would someone want to set up a company way out here in the boon-docks?

His curiosity enticed him to approach the building. A small light glowed over the front door revealing a security keypad as well as an intercom button.

Alex pressed the button once.

It seemed to take forever before the front door finally opened. A man of medium height stood in the door frame. "Hello. Can I help you?" he said politely to Alex.

"Good evening. My name is Alex Wiley. I live up the road and was curious about the development of this property. Would you mind if I had a look around?" Peter shook Alex's hand and replied, "Not at all. Come on in. My name is Peter Preston by the way. I am the owner of this place." He laughed lightly.

Peter began to briefly explain to Alex the nature of his project without going into too much detail. "Do you have an interest in computers?" Peter asked Alex casually.

"As I matter of fact I do. I have a degree in computer engineering from Bayport University. To be honest though, I've never worked in the field. I've been helping my dad run our family business. Maybe you've heard of it. Wiley Industries?"

"Office supplies, right?" responded Peter pointing a finger jovially at Alex.

"You got it. But lately I've been considering doing something else ... before my computer skills get too rusty."

Peter laughed. "That can happen."

Once this common denominator was established between the two men they became more comfortable with each other. Peter took Alex on a tour through the renovated factory. After months of secrecy it was a relief for Peter to speak openly about his invention DIM. And, for some reason, he found it easy to talk to Alex about the secret project.

As they went through the various areas of the factory Peter explained what would be done once the company was in operation. "I'm in the process of hiring for the company now."

Alex was raised in a business environment, having been a part of the Wiley family business since he was sixteen years old. He recognized an opportunity when he saw one. He knew that if a person didn't seize an opportunity it would float away and benefit someone else. He could see one opening right now. "Would you consider hiring a novice computer engineer ... say on a trial basis?"

Peter stopped to consider the idea. *A computer engineer might make a great part of the design team.*

He asked Alex to drop off a resume with two references. He promised he would get back to him the following week. "How does that sound?" Peter smiled encouragingly.

"Sounds great! Thanks for considering me," Alex said appreciatively. The two men shook hands sealing the friendship.

CHAPTER 13

Ethel Dingledine was a past student of Professor Preston. She was tall and gangly with black frizzy hair. During her years as a student she and Peter had become close friends. When Peter decided to confide in her about his plans to start a company, she immediately offered her assistance. "Just name it. I would be happy to help."

Ethel was now busy preparing the conference room at the shared executive office for interviews that would take place in the afternoon. Peter had booked the room for the entire day. In one corner of the conference room Ethel set up a refreshments table with coffee, tea, orange juice, and a basket of fresh muffins. It was her duty to act as hostess and provide general assistance to Peter while he did the job interviews.

The first prospective employee arrived at one o'clock. Sticking to a list of questions he had prepared the previous day, Peter began the arduous process of interviewing each candidate in hopes of finding suitable personnel for DIM Inc.

During the interview Peter jotted notes onto a form. Later, he planned to rate each candidate on a scale from one to ten for suitability. Realizing he would not be able to remember everyone afterwards he needed to make a tentative decision during the actual interview.

One candidate for one of the factory positions was a friendly fellow named Bill Hoggart who had once worked for *Hidden Valley Railway*. Peter liked him instantly. They spent a good ten minutes talking about the "good old days" when rail travel was popular. Even though Bill wasn't very well educated he had a lot of experience that might come in handy in a factory setting. Peter placed a red checkmark at the top of his questionnaire form to remind himself to consider hiring the man.

Another candidate was a stunningly beautiful woman named Julie Sanders. Peter warmed up to her immediately. She was easy to talk to and knew a lot about the software industry. She was honest with Peter about her lost job at GameSoft due to downsizing. He believed her invaluable experience and insight might prove beneficial to his technology business.

By the end of the first day of interviews Peter was completely energized from talking to so many different people. He knew he wouldn't be able to sleep a wink that night. But at least he now had a list of competent candidates to choose from.

After the last applicant left, Peter asked Ethel to have dinner with him. "Would you like to go out for a spaghetti dinner, Ethel? It's the least I can offer you after your help today." Ethel agreed providing she could pick the restaurant. They locked up the office and headed to *Romeos* for dinner.

*   *   *

One week later Peter had made his final selection for the personnel he wished to hire for DIM Inc. Out of the forty people he had interviewed, twenty-five were rated acceptable. From there he narrowed the choices down to actual hirelings. Peter decided it would be wise to keep a waiting list in case he needed to hire more staff in the future.

He telephoned each successful candidate and offered them their position personally and gave a start date. He promised to mail a map giving directions to the factory's location. All the candidates he called accepted the job offer. This secretly pleased Peter and made him feel positive about his choices.

For the candidates that were not selected Peter sent each one a polite regrets letter. He felt it was a good idea to maintain professionalism even in a negative situation.

Now, with the old building renovated, the assembly line ready for production, and the initial personnel hired, the green light came on; DIM was ready to come to life.

CHAPTER 14

August 1st 9:00 a.m.

Day one of the New Beginnings sessions

Monday morning is traditionally the first day of the workweek for most companies so it only seemed natural for Peter Preston to start his new company on a Monday morning.

Peter set up the boardroom as a teaching unit. Here he planned to give a short lecture each day of the first week to introduce the new design team to the company, the product, the policies and procedures, as well their individual instructions for their new positions. Once the design team was underway Peter planned to introduce the remaining personnel to the company.

A three-foot white melamine board was mounted on one of the walls in the boardroom. Next to it stood an easel full of posters and charts of varying sizes all relating to the DIM project. Hanging on the walls of the boardroom were motivational prints with messages of encouragement like: *No Pain No Gain, Learn & Earn,* and *Success Is A Step in the Right Direction.* A brass showcase lamp, similar to those used in art galleries, illuminated the prints with a soft glow.

In the center of the boardroom was a sectional table with four equal parts that fit together like a giant puzzle. Around this table were ten purple armless coaster chairs. The table gave the room a sense of purpose.

In one corner of the boardroom was a royal palm planted in a painted clay pot. The branches occasionally fluttered from the breeze made by the lazy spinning of an overhead industrial fan.

Outside the boardroom were hospitality offerings including: gourmet coffee and tea, English muffins, and fruit punch. At the back of the cloth-covered table was a sterling silver bucket filled with crushed ice.

Far above in the rafters of the ceiling came the sounds of mellow music. A stereo system with speakers had been installed throughout the building to provide many hours of easy-listening music for the benefit of the workers.

On this first official day as owner of DIM Inc. Peter chose to abandon his former conservative attire and go with a more contemporary look. He wore a green suit with wide cuffs and a single button in the center of the jacket. The shirt was gray silk. The tie had tiny computers on it.

By ten o'clock in the morning the design team trio was seated at the boardroom table. Each one had a pad of paper in front of them. Like Peter they too were dressed professionally and ready to begin with a positive start.

Peter stood at the head of the table. "Good morning. As you already know, my name is Peter Preston and I am the owner of DIM Inc. My company will be making a *portable research computer*. You are here to assist in the development of the commercial prototype."

Where most new business owners might be nervous at a time

like this Peter wasn't edgy in the least. During his years as a professor he had faced many groups of people. Public speaking came naturally to him.

"I would like to introduce each of you to the other members of the design team. First ... let me introduce Melanie Gold. Melanie is the owner of Gold Advertising which is a desktop-publishing firm located here in Greenvale. She has graciously offered her services to this project. Melanie's main task will be to design the external appearance of the DIM computer. She will also be assisting in designing marketing material."

Melanie stood up and said "Hello" to the other two team members.

Peter went on to the second team member. "This is Alex Wiley. Alex comes from a well-known family in Greenvale and happens to live nearby. Alex has a degree in computer engineering from Bayport University. He will be responsible for designing the hardware components of the DIM computer. Please welcome him to our team."

There was another round of friendly hellos.

Peter turned to the smiling face of Julie Sanders who was obviously pleased to be employed once more. She sat across the table from Alex and Melanie with her back as straight as a ruler. "This is Julie Sanders and she will be our software programmer. Julie will be developing the programming for the DIM computer. She has five years experience in this field and I am confident that she will do a first-rate job here at DIM Inc."

After this round of introductions Peter approached the

melamine board. Using a blue dry-erase marker, he began to make a list of the topics he planned to discuss that week.

"I would like to give a short lecture each morning this week. This will help introduce you to the project. You will learn more about the company, the product, and the policies and procedures. You will also be given individual instructions for your particular tasks.

"Today, we will be discussing your contracts and the general rules of the company."

Peter handed each team member a portfolio containing their contracts, a policies & procedures manual, and a job description for each position. He asked the design team to spend a few minutes reviewing the material.

While the trio scanned the info Peter went to the easel and sifted through the charts until he found the one he was looking for. He placed it at the front. The heading read: PAYMENT PLAN.

Gaining the attention of the design team once more he explained the payment plan. "I have hired each of you to perform a particular task. These tasks all relate to the development of a prototype for the commercial DIM computer. Once this prototype is complete your services will no longer be required ... *however* ... (Peter paused) ... because these tasks are *so* vital to the success of the company I feel you deserve more financial compensation than just a salary." He stopped to take a sip of Earl-Grey tea from his mug.

"In your portfolios you will notice a certificate made out to each of you. This is a profit-sharing certificate. It entitles you to receive 2% of the gross revenue of DIM Inc. ... beginning the first month that sales are made ... and ending exactly five years from that date. You will receive this payment in a separate deposit in your bank account on the fifteenth day of each month. As long as the company remains in operation, and as long as it is making sales, this payment will be made to you."

A murmur of appreciation came from the design trio.

"The purpose of this payment is to act as an incentive. I want you to put your best effort into making a superb prototype of DIM. If you make it fantastic, you will help the company succeed, and in turn, this profit-sharing payment will be your reward. This is only fair ... in my opinion ... since it will be *your* ingenuity that is likely to make or break the business."

Peter selected a copy of the employment contract from a sample of forms on the table in front of him. "This is a copy of your employment contract stating the terms and conditions of your employment here at DIM Inc. I would like you to read it over carefully. If you are satisfied with it, and agree to the terms, sign it and return it to me before you leave today. If you have any discrepancies, pencil them in, and I will review them with you later. Once the contracts are signed, a copy will be given to you for your records."

Peter gave the team a chance to glance over their contracts before continuing with his discussion. "One of the conditions of your employment is to keep everything about the company a secret. This is a *mandatory* requirement. I will be explaining the reasons *why* when we discuss the strategy plan on Thursday.

"You will be allowed to set your own work time schedule. Apart from pre-arranged meetings, such as this one, you may work any time you wish between the hours of seven a.m. and nine at night ... any day of the week.

"Your flat-rate hourly fee will be $30 per hour. This salary is in addition to the profit-sharing payment I might add. You must submit your time sheets to the bookkeeper by five o'clock on Friday if you want to be paid the following Wednesday.

"Each of you will be given a security card and a passcode to access the front door of this building. This door will be kept locked at all times so don't forget to bring it with you. If you *do* get locked out there is an intercom buzzer outside the door. I can't guarantee anyone will answer but give it a try anyway," Peter chuckled.

"Dress code is casual. This is an old building so please dress warmly. You might want to leave a sweater or jacket here. There are lockers in the lunchroom. No jeans, t-shirts, or running shoes though — not that casual.

"Once we are finished here, today, I will show you to your workstations. Please make yourselves at home. Before leaving each day tidy your work areas. Remember, some of the material you will be working on could become extremely valuable one day. There is a fireproof safe in the bookkeeper's office. You are welcome to use it for storing important documents ... or anything else you think is worth safeguarding. Any questions?"

The design team expressed satisfaction with their working conditions and agreed to the terms of the employment contract. One of their concerns, however, was how long the project would last.

"My guess is a year or more. Is that OK with you?" Peter asked.

"As long as I can work on a part-time basis, I have no

objection," Melanie affirmed. "I do have obligations to my clients."

By four o'clock all the contracts were signed and copies made. Peter thanked each member of the design team for joining the company. On a last note he urged them, "Give this project your best effort. Make the prototype of DIM a technological sensation. I want it to knock the socks off our customers. It can't just be good — it has to be great!"

CHAPTER 15

August 2nd 9:00 a.m.

Day two of the New Beginnings sessions

"DIM means ... *data-interpreter module.*" Peter Preston wrote the name in full on the melamine board. Today he planned to discuss the features of DIM and give a general overview of the personal research computer.

"It is called this because data is retrieved from the computer's memory banks by entering keywords. The results of the search are then presented to the operator in a customized format."

It seemed to Peter that whenever he talked about technology in research it gave him a burst of enthusiasm. It was one of his favorite topics.

"DIM is a portable research computer. It will be a PC-like unit with a large memory capable of storing information useful to the researcher. DIM could also be viewed as a *digital reference library.*"

Peter approached the sketch of a DIM model displayed on the easel. Picking up a twelve-inch pointer stick he pointed to the sketch.

"As you can see from this drawing, DIM will be a one-piece unit with a 17-inch monitor. Here is the Power button. This slot is where you can insert a USB flash-drive to download data. And this slot here is where you can insert a CD. On the right side of the unit will be a built-in printer that will use rolls of fax paper." Peter pointed to each area of the diagram as he spoke.

"In the opening screen the operator will enter in the keywords. This tells DIM what information to look for on the hard-drive. DIM's search utility will then find passages of text that contain *all* of those keywords.

"Data can be retrieved from any drive. It is like having the reference section of a library accessible from a single source. You see, one of the problems with manual researching is the researcher has to hunt all over the place for pertinent information. It can take hours to locate facts because you have to look things up in so many different resources to find relevant items. With DIM these resources will be available on the computer."

Alex interrupted Peter, "So ... you're saying ... the main goal of doing research with a DIM computer will be as a time-saver."

"Exactly!" agreed Peter. "With a DIM computer you can search a topic, view the passages, and print the results, all in just a few minutes. The same process in manual researching would take you several hours, even days, from my experience. This valuable time could be better spent than pouring through books and magazines in a library."

Peter sorted through a stack of charts and brought one forward that said: FEATURES OF DIM.

"This chart shows you a list of what DIM's main features will be. You can use this list as a guide when you are developing the commercial prototype."

"The ten main features of DIM are as follows:

"Feature 1. DIM will have a memory capacity of 5 terabytes.

"Feature 2. Only DIM's built-in software that comes with the computer will be permitted on the hard-drive. No external software programs can be downloaded.

"Feature 3. Data can be loaded onto the hard-drive as text or graphic images. A hand-held scanner will also be included, as an accessory, for storing images in the database.

"Feature 4. The keyboard of the computer will be customized to perform DIM functions only. It will not resemble the traditional computer keyboard.

"Feature 5. Each DIM computer will come with a selection of pre-loaded databases.

"Feature 6. In addition to the default databases, an operator can download their own databases to the hard-drive via the ports.

"Feature 7. The search results can be printed. There will be a built-in printer on the side of the computer which uses a roll of paper.

"Feature 8. There will be a maximum of ten search summaries per screen. The search summary will include: the source of the passage, the author of the text (if applicable), and the first two lines of the actual passage.

"Feature 9. Up to ten keywords can be used for performing a search. A keyword can be one word or a group of words. All of the keywords must be found in a passage for it to be shown in the search results. This helps reduce the number of results presented in the search summary.

"Feature 10. The most significant of DIM's features will be the text-block-range. The operator must specify the size of the block of the text that the keywords are to be found in. A text-block can be as small as 10 words or it can be as large as 500 words.

"Are you getting the general gist of what this product will be?" Peter asked the design team.

Each one nodded.

Peter continued, "I know it is hard to imagine what the computer will be able to do ... without actually seeing one in action."

Alex asked, "Are you wanting us to create a prototype based on these features?"

Peter replied, "Essentially, yes, although there is definitely room for your ideas. Years ago I had a model of DIM and it worked very well. Unfortunately it was stolen from one of my classes. I can guide you through the process. It won't be difficult."

Julie piped in. "I agree. The basic concept is not that complicated. The technology is there too. I'm looking forward to the challenge of doing the prototype."

"So am I," said Melanie.

The design team agreed to meet back at the factory the same time the next day

CHAPTER 16

Day three of the New Beginnings sessions

Julie asked, "Who do you anticipate will use a DIM computer?"

Peter answered, "I'm hoping the product will be used by many different types of people. Once the public becomes familiar with the computer's basic operation they may discover their own uses for it. This, hopefully, will make DIM popular. The most obvious users of DIM would be researchers. So this would appeal to students and writers.

"A business owner might find DIM beneficial when they can do custom searches of specialized databases for their particular business. For example, a health-care professional could use DIM to help diagnose an illness of a sick patient by searching a database of medical ailments and their corresponding treatments. The possibilities are endless in my opinion," Peter concluded.

Julie said, "So it is possible that DIM might be marketable to many different customers each using it for their own purposes."

"That's what I'm hoping for." Peter relaxed against his chair. "I realize that anything new takes to time to become known. However, I believe if we emphasize the *uses* of DIM in our promotions ... it should catch on."

Melanie said dreamily, "It's kind of a writer's dream-come-true isn't it? To be able to quickly look up something in your own electronic library would save a lot of trips to the public library."

Peter smiled. "Now your the getting the idea. This computer is versatile. No two users would use DIM for the same two reasons. That's the beauty of it. After all what does any one person use a library for? There are thousands of reasons why a person might use a library. DIM is a simply a digital library they can access at home or in their workplace."

On a practical level Alex said, "Do you anticipate many businesses would want to invest in one of the DIM computers since most people already have PC's?"

"Certainly," answered Peter with confidence. "It will be affordable. It will come with a step-by-step manual. Once they figure out how DIM will be a benefit in their business I'm certain they'll never regret their investment in buying one."

"How much would a DIM computer cost?" Melanie inquired. She knew the price would ultimately determine the company's success.

Peter turned to her. "To make DIM a marketable product I'm guessing it would have to sell for less than $500. I am hoping for a $300 price range with deluxe models costing a bit more of course. What is your opinion?"

Melanie agreed. "If it costs more than a normal PC you might put yourself out of the market. But at $300 you might sell a lot of them. That's cheap enough for someone who wants to try it out."

Julie interjected, "Let's make them beautiful to look at. Most computers are so dreary looking. They are always black, beige or gray. How dull! If we make the DIM computers stand out they are sure to get noticed."

"That's a good suggestion!" Alex piped in.

Peter said, "This is why I hired you. I want you to make the DIM computer a sensation. Hold nothing back in your imagination. Make it a technological masterpiece. Even make the how-to manual perfect. When people know how to *use* DIM, in as many situations as possible, then — and only then — will we be in business!"

CHAPTER 17

Wiley Estate, Hidden Valley, 6 p.m.

"You did what?!!!" roared James Wiley like a lion who had just been let out of his cage for the first time in years. He went livid when he discovered his son Alex had cancelled most of his business commitments with Wiley Industries to work on a secret project as a computer engineer.

Alex faced his furious father in the living room of their colonial home. "It's only for a short time, father ... maybe a couple of months." Alex tried to appease the raging lion by making light of the situation. He had no intention of telling his father that the project might actually go on for a year or more.

"Why now, Alex?" James began to pace back and forth in front of the fireplace huffing and puffing in annoyance. James Wiley was sure he had nipped Alex's degree in the bud years ago. Obviously he hadn't done as good a job as he thought.

Alex sat on the arm of a nearby chair remaining tight-lipped. This wasn't the first time he had seen his father go into a rage. These angry outbursts were one of traits that Alex did not like about his father including one where his father never admitted when he was wrong. In all the years Alex had known his father, he had never once heard Wiley Sr. apologize to anyone for anything.

Alex decided to take the offensive. "Why do you have to be the only decision-maker? I am a member of this family too. Or haven't you noticed?" His voice was dredged with sarcasm. He got up from his chair and started walking towards the door.

"I haven't finished with you yet!" bellowed James Wiley.

Alex spun around and met his father's angry gaze with an eye-to-eye glare of combat. "I am thirty-five years old — and if I wish to make a decision regarding my own life — without consulting you — I will do so! I don't give a damn whether you approve of my plans or not. This is something *I* want to do." He sucked in a deep breath in an attempt to control his own mounting rage.

In spite of his father's pessimistic attitude, Alex had no intention of changing his mind regarding his commitment to DIM Inc. It was the first time in years he had felt positive about what he was doing.

"Not when it concerns the Wiley family business," James's voice suddenly dropped an octave lower into a deadly tone. "You have your responsibilities to Wiley Industries. You can't just ignore them. I will not allow you to shirk your duties onto the shoulders of the employees. And don't think I haven't noticed you doing this recently. I've received several reports from top personnel about some *unauthorized* changes you have made."

"I am not shirking by responsibilities!" Alex lashed back. "I admit I have allocated some tasks to other staff members in the office ... to Ian Sullivan, for example. By the way Ian is a lot more capable than you give him credit for. I plan to free up most of my time to devote to the computer project I am working on ..."

James interrupted with a phony smile. "What *is* this secret project you are working on, by the way?"

Alex hesitated. Instinctively he knew it wouldn't be wise to tell his father any details about the new company. "I'm sorry but I can't tell you. I have signed a confidentiality agreement. It forbids me to discuss the project with outsiders." Alex smirked at his father. "You'll have to wait until the project is finished."

"Outsiders, my foot!" His father threw up his arms in a gesture of exasperation. "I give up!" James's face went beet-red. "You have it your way, Alex, but if these new career plans of yours fail ... don't come crying to me to bail you out. You're on your own with this one."

Before Alex could respond his father stormed passed him and out the living room slamming the door behind him. The sound of the reverberating glass echoed throughout the room.

Alex collapsed backwards into a nearby chair. "Whew!" he said out loud with relief, "I'm glad that's over with."

The new DIM project was too exciting to give up yet. It had all the adventure his life needed right now. Furthermore, it was saving his hard-earned education from being permanently shelved. *Was there anything wrong with that?*

CHAPTER 18

Greenvale Railway Station, 8:20 am

Peter stood in the ticket line at the Greenvale train station. When he approached the wicket, he set his briefcase and overnight bag down beside him, and pulled out his wallet.

"A return to Bayport, please," Peter said to the ticket agent.

"That will be 36 dollars and 75 cents." The ticket agent wore a navy blue jacket with a gold nameplate that said: ROSS - TICKET AGENT.

Peter paid the agent and received his train ticket in a silver folder. He put the folder in the inside pocket of his jacket, tucked his wallet away, picked up his bags, and headed for Platform 2 where a westbound train was waiting.

Bursts of hot steam hissed out from under the train as Peter walked along the platform. Stepping on a yellow footstool he boarded the first-class coach at the front of the train.

Peter chose a window seat on the right side of the train. He stored his overnight bag in the overhead compartment but kept his briefcase down beside him. He settled in the comfortable recliner seat waiting for departure.

He was heading to Bayport to meet Henri Larue, the newly-hired marketing manager of DIM Inc. This meeting would initiate the ad campaign that would launch the new computers. It was to be an open discussion where both could hash out ideas on how to market the product.

At the rear of the coach one of the train porters called out, "All aboard!" After three short whistles and a long one the train began to inch its way down the track and out of the station.

Five minutes later a conductor came down the aisle and politely requested Peter's ticket. Deftly tearing off one portion the conductor handed the receipt portion back to Peter and said, "Have a pleasant journey, sir."

The train jugged across the flat plain of Hidden Valley heading towards the western hills. From the window of the train the scenery was spectacular. They passed over a narrow bridge above Snake River. The train slowed to a crawl. Peter was presented with a view of the river five hundred feet below. He watched the rushing waters dance around giant boulders as the river snaked its way through the course it had made hundreds of years ago.

As the train left the valley it traveled through a five-mile tunnel called *The Deathtrap* by local railroad personnel. The darkness inside the tunnel was a sharp contrast to the brilliance of the morning daylight. The sound of the train grew louder and louder with squeaky wheels and whistles echoing off the tunnel walls. It seemed to take forever before they finally emerged out the other side.

Only green could be seen as they passed through forests on their way to the city of Bayport. Farms here and there showed signs of sporadic civilization making it seem unlikely their final destination would be to a city of two million people.

The preliminary marketing meetings were to be held in the waterfront office located in Bayport. Unlike the somewhat gloomy atmosphere of the factory, the marketing offices in Bayport were prestigious and cheerful. The professor had purposely chosen a penthouse suite of offices in a deluxe office building to impress the company's clients and make them think the business was already booming.

Henri Larue had come recommended to Peter through an advertising agency in Bayport. According to his portfolio, Henri had helped several other companies achieve the ten-million-dollar mark in sales. Much of these successes were attributed to Larue's ingenuity. There was no doubt about it; he was a marketing whiz.

Henri employed a combination of contemporary marketing techniques with a few reliable secrets he had learned from the old school of marketing. Now, thanks to his clever campaigns, one of the companies he had helped launch was grossing a cool one hundred million dollars annually.

After studying his impressive portfolio Peter felt confident that Henri's talents in marketing would prove beneficial to DIM Inc. So he hired him on the spot with a two-year contract.

Peter read over the notes he had prepared the night before. He added a few items to the agenda and crossed off a couple he thought they wouldn't have time for. This preliminary set of meetings would likely last two or three days depending on much they accomplished.

Half-an-hour later Peter put away his briefcase and slept lightly for the remainder of the train trip.

*   *   *

At precisely 10:45 a.m. the train pulled into Bayport Central Station. Peter disembarked and followed the crowd down the narrow stairwell to the grand lobby below. The train station was a famous landmark in the city. Built in the days of deluxe train travel the station reflected former days of prosperity. It retained original hand-painted murals on a dome-shaped ceiling. There were six enormous white pillars that rose up to the roof. Small souvenir shops did a great business selling to tourists, visitors, and homecoming Bayport residents.

When Peter got to the end of the brass railing he easily spotted Henri Larue waiting patiently at the roped-off entranceway. He waved at him.

Henri was in his mid-forties, had brown hair and a moustache. He was of medium build and wore a grey charcoal suit. The two men shook hands and exchanged greetings. They made their way up the marble stairs to the busy street above.

Henri Larue's white ambassador-style car was parked in a metered zone only a short distance from the station. They got into the car and drove down Danby Street towards the harbor.

Bayport had once been a busy port serving both cargo and passenger ships. But since the shipping industry had declined the port activity diminished. Now only occasional ships came in to deliver or receive goods.

Many of the buildings along the waterfront were no longer warehouses storing cargo from ships. Most of them had been renovated and turned into fancy office space. These offices were available for lease at high rates. In recent years the waterfront had become a chic spot for both business and tourism. There was an art gallery as well as many upscale cafés and expensive restaurants.

Henri's father was French but his mother was English. This gave him the advantage of knowing both languages equally fluently. Since Peter's French was a little rusty, they agreed to speak in English.

"Were you able to get the office furnished?" Peter inquired.

"Yes I did. My wife helped with the color schemes. The interior decorator did the final touches last Friday. I must say it looks terrific. And it didn't cost that much either."

Henri spun his car with expertise into a parking lot across the street from the building where the marketing office was located. As he got out of the car Henri laughed and said to Peter, "The only disadvantage with this parking lot is that it sometimes takes me five whole minutes just to cross the street. Harbor Boulevard has got to be the busiest street in town. I would use the lights only they are two blocks away."

When the two men finally crossed the traffic-laden street they entered a five-storey building with white stucco siding and blue glass windows. Stopping in at the security desk Peter greeted the guard and explained the purpose of his visit.

They walked along a navy carpet runner leading to a luxurious set of mirrored elevators. "This really is a nice building, isn't it?" commented Peter as the elevator doors silently opened and allowed them to enter.

"Real classy. And clean too." Henri remarked.

The penthouse suite of offices was on the fifth floor of the building. When they arrived the elevator door opened to a wide corridor.

They soon stood in front of a set of double-glass doors with the words etched in bold black letters: R.T.E. - MARKETING & PROMOTIONS. Henri swiped his pass card through the electronic device beside the door. The door clicked open.

Peter felt like a king walking into a palace as they entered the suite. Purple and mauve were the dominant colors of the ostentatious office. A dark-purple leather sofa spelled luxury and comfort. In front of the sofa was a smoky-colored glass table with an ebony frame. Sitting in the center of the table was a live orchid plant with six pink blooms hanging from delicate vines. Next to the planter was a selection of recent issues of business magazines. Various prints portraying famous inventions adorned the walls of the reception area. The room had a subtle sensual masculine appeal.

"What's that nice smell?" Peter asked Henri.

"Oh it's a plug-in fragrance behind the sofa. My wife put it there. She said it is supposed to smell like lotus flowers." He chuckled.

Peter said, "I'm not sure what lotus flowers are supposed to smell like, but it does smell nice."

The marketing offices of DIM Inc. were actually a suite of three rooms. The room the men had just entered was a reception and meeting area. It was here they would hold their meetings to discuss the marketing plans for the new company.

A side door to the left led to a working office with four dividers separating functional workstations. There was a computer on each desk and a small filing cabinet beside it. At the far end of this long rectangular room was a storage room equipped with a security lock system. In this tiny windowless room there was equipment for creating microfiche files.

After a quick tour of the office suite Peter went and stood in front of the floor-to-ceiling window. It provided a magnificent view of the harbor. He had a birds-eye view of the crowds of people below walking along the boardwalk. He could see two ships, countless shops, and a steady stream of traffic. It was a stimulating sight.

Peter felt almost reluctant to start the meeting; he was enjoying the view so much. "I guess we better get started ... if we want to make any headway today."

"Sure," Henri replied in an agreeable manner. He hustled over to the conference room table and began to set up at one end of the table.

Peter spread his notes out in front of him with the agenda on top. "I plan to stay in Bayport for a couple of days. I've made an agenda of items I want to discuss ... but this is just a rough guide. Feel free to add your own items to this list."

"OK." Henri took it. "Let me take a look at it."

Both Henri and Peter had ideas on how to promote the new product. Henri sat across from Peter at the conference table each with a fresh cup of coffee.

Henri spoke earnestly. "My initial marketing plan for DIM is to do a *television infomercial*. They are especially effective when introducing a virtually unknown product onto the market."

"An infomercial?" Peter immediately perked up. It was an idea he had not yet thought of. He was expecting Henri to suggest a magazine ad or a company brochure or something familiar like that. "Go on ... I'm listening."

Henri continued, "An infomercial can reach a huge audience in a short space of time. Millions of people watch the shopping channels every day. People are always on the look out for new products. You wouldn't believe how many people are curious to try something out ... just because it's new and saw it on TV.

"Television infomercials are the best way to show someone *how* to use a product because you can give a live demonstration. No other advertising method can do this. In half-an-hour you can tell someone more about a product than you can with a hundred magazine ads. In my opinion an infomercial would be the ideal way to introduce DIM to the public."

"Henri, that's a *great* idea!" Peter slapped the top of the conference table. He was extremely pleased. Like a passing storm cloud showing a sunny blue sky behind it, Peter could now see a future for his company emerging.

"What will it cost?" Peter was already sold on the idea.

Henri wanted Peter to be aware of the benefits and the drawbacks of the infomercial scheme. "I should warn you it will cost more than a series of magazine ads but we will probably recover the costs more quickly ... through instant sales. You see, after people see an infomercial they generally call up the 800# or go to the website address right away. Their enthusiasm translates into immediate sales. This doesn't usually happen with magazine ads since there is not the same sense of urgency to purchase."

Peter himself had watched the occasional infomercial on television. His favorite products were sporting goods. He knew from personal experience some of the products were superbly designed. All of them were relatively inexpensive — compared to products sold in retail stores. This was due to the low overhead costs of direct-factory sales. Peter also knew infomercials could bring in tremendous revenue as a result of word-of-mouth referrals.

Peter showed his support, "I think it would be worth the investment. Can we do more than one?"

"Absolutely. Once the pilot for the show is complete it can become an ongoing promotional tool. You will receive discounts from the television station when you air an infomercial more than once. It is cheaper if you run the infomercial after midnight too."

Henri handed Peter a brochure providing details about making an infomercial. "Here is a cost breakdown for doing an infomercial. Perhaps we can talk the design team into helping, instead of hiring actors. This would save us some money. As you can see from the price-list actors are quite expensive."

"Good. I'll ask them," Peter replied and jotted a note down on a pad of paper.

Henri told Peter he had done an infomercial before with another company. "How to order the product is the secret to getting more sales from an infomercial. We need to provide *several* easy ways to order the product. Because DIM is a technology product, an online ordering system at an e-commerce website would be appropriate. I notice a lot of companies are weak in this area. They think all you need is an 800# and everything will take care of itself. Not true. Online sales are better than telephone sales because you can reach millions of people around the world twenty-four hours a day, seven days a week. That will give us tremendous sales potential. You can't run a phone service for that amount of time without it costing you a fortune. Trust me, I know."

Peter suddenly had an idea. "What if we automate the entire telephone sales procedure? Then we would only need to hire people to translate the calls into messages. Then we could run both the 800# service and the e-commerce site 24/7."

"Good idea. That would work." Henri said. "Let's say someone wants to buy a DIM computer but they want it *now*. They don't want to wait six to eight weeks for delivery. So ... we provide them with an option to have delivery by *courier*. They would pay extra of course but then this would guarantee they could get their computer within two or three days."

Peter responded excitedly, "Excellent suggestion. Since we will be doing only direct-factory sales it would be a plus to offer courier-delivery service, at the customer's expense, as you say."

Things were going well at this marketing meeting. Both Peter and Henri were committed to making DIM an overnight success. They pooled their ideas together and planned how to make them work.

At the end of the day they locked up the office and left. Henri dropped Peter off at the *Waterfront Inn* where Peter had reservations for a two-night stay.

"Shall I pick you up at eight tomorrow morning?" Henri asked.

"Sounds good to me. I'll be waiting in the lobby," smiled Peter.

He waved and disappeared through the revolving doors of the lakeshore hotel.

CHAPTER 19

The design team hovered around Alex's draftsman's table in the administrative area at the factory. They were reviewing the plans for the commercial prototype of DIM.

"It is only a matter of synchronizing our ideas and then the test-model can be made," Alex explained.

"How long do you think it will take to do it?" asked Melanie who wasn't familiar with the process of creating prototypes.

"Maybe two months," Alex guessed. "Three at the most."

The design trio scanned the notes silently.

"I've been thinking about what Julie said about the color of the units," Melanie broke through the quiet spell. "First I thought we should make them bright cheery colors ... like red or yellow ... you know, to get them noticed. But then I realized that might make them look childish. It would be better if the DIM computers appear to be more professional since most of the customers are likely to be business people or educators. So then I had this idea. What about *oyster-shell* which is a blend of gray, blue, and red? It's more exotic than beige or grey but it is still fairly conservative."

Julie agreed. "I say good choice. It would present a nice image too by symbolizing DIM as a pearl inside an oyster."

Alex offered his opinion. "An oyster-shell color would suit

both male and female users alike. It is kind of a non-partisan color."

Melanie agreed. "Yes, that's important."

Julie had been working on some ideas for the software. "Everyone is familiar with search engines on the Internet. When people are accustomed to doing something in a certain way they are more likely to accept a new idea easier if it is done in a similar manner. So I thought we should make the search results in DIM resemble the results you get when you do an online search. The passage title would be in blue text and underlined. The description area would be the first two lines of the passage. The keywords would be shown in bold text. The general layout would be identical to the results of a search engine. They should catch on to using DIM quicker this way."

"You're right!" Alex exclaimed. "A familiar-looking screen would make a user feel more comfortable in trying out DIM."

Julie continued, "When the user clicks on the passage link they will be taken to the actual passage in the database — like on the Internet when the user is taken to a website. Then the user would scroll down the screen while they read the passage the same way they would scroll down a webpage.

Julie continued, "I decided this would make it easier to train people on how to use their DIM computer."

"It would." Alex was impressed. "People are already familiar with search engines so they'll catch on to the DIM computer ... if it is laid out in a similar style, as you say. Good thinking!" Alex gave Julie a thumbs-up sign.

Julie smiled at him. "Thanks, Alex."

The pros and cons of doing repairs on faulty computers were

also discussed. The trio came to the conclusion that it was too expensive to train servicemen to do repairs and too much hassle. Instead they would recommend to Peter that only product replacements be done for the occasional faulty computer. Broken computers would then be returned to the factory where they would be dismantled and the parts recycled. This seemed to be a logical and cost-effective solution to an occasional problem.

Alex laid out his own plan. "Once DIM has been assembled I suggest we coat the inner components completely with a centimeter or so of molten neon plastic. When this plastic hardens it will form a coating which will serve as a protection to the internal components of the computer against any excessive physical movements — like dropping the unit. Even though this may not happen very often, it would reduce the number of units needing to be replaced.

Alex continued, "This plastic coating will also give the computer some measure of security protection from hackers and such because it would hide the design of the hardware from prying eyes."

Melanie asked, "But wouldn't the plastic stop the air from circulating inside the machine ... and cause heat to build up?"

Alex replied, "Yes it would. But if we put small circulation tunnels for the fan to blow air through ... heat build-up shouldn't become a problem. Once we have the prototype done I will leave a unit on for a week and then test it for heat build-up ... just to make sure."

Julie knew a lot about piracy in the technology industry from her work experience at GameSoft. "A sealed component might make it more difficult to create a clone of DIM ... but not necessarily impossible. Any company that *does* manage to create a clone of DIM could run off with the bulk of Peter's business."

"Let's ask Peter if we can discuss security measures at our next design meeting," Alex made a note in his daily planner.

The design team set the deadline for the completion of the prototype of DIM for October 31st.

CHAPTER 20

Around noon the following day Peter and Henri walked along the boardwalk of the Bayport Harbor looking for a good place to eat lunch. The jetty was crowded with tourists. All the outdoor cafés were filled to capacity with people enjoying their meal underneath colorful patio umbrellas. Dozens of seagulls came in to land on the peer ledge hoping to catch a scrap of food.

"I read somewhere there are more than three million tourists that visit the Bayport wharf area every year. You can tell how popular it is." Henri spoke as they fought their way through the crowd.

Eventually they found a vacant table at *Crêpes de Jour* one of the restaurants along the wharf. "You don't mind French cooking do you?" Henri asked Peter.

"Not at all."

They ordered ham & cheese crepes, Caesar salads, and a couple of bottles of Heineken beer. They agreed to use this business lunch to discuss the strategy plan Peter had developed for the company. Peter wasn't sure how well Henri would accept the plan so he approached the subject surreptitiously.

"Fifty years ago a corporate strategy plan would probably not have been necessary for a new business," Peter began as he took a sip of beer. "But with all the mergers and acquisitions going on today I think one is *vital* now. Any business owner today who doesn't recognize the dangers of takeovers is just plain irresponsible."

Henri was wise to the ways of the business world and readily agreed these were dangers to guard against. "You're right, Peter. Takeovers are happening more and more frequently. What do you have in mind?"

"I created a strategy plan to try and protect the company from a possible takeover. You must realize it is meant as a precautionary measure only." Peter began to outline the points of his strategy plan.

"Confidentiality about everything relating to the company will be mandatory for all personnel of DIM Inc. Anyone who exposes facts or details about the business will be dismissed. I realize this sounds over-reactive but it is a vital key in my plan.

"The second part is for *your* area, Henri. We will not be doing any media interviews ... at least not until DIM Inc. is well established. You might consider this to be a bad marketing move but we must remain as publicly invisible for as long as possible. We need to make it difficult for any person to track us down."

Henri's eyebrows shot up. "No interviews?"

"That's right. In my opinion interviews only do a little bit of good in the early stages of a business but they can do a lot of harm by exposing details about a new company to people who don't need to know about us. Does a customer really need to know my name, what university I attended, or where I live, to be confident in making a purchase of a DIM computer? I think not. All they need to know is what the product can do for them, how to order it, and how to get customer service. I want us to keep silent in everything else. Once we are doing well then we can start spreading the word through publicity interviews."

Peter glanced around him as if someone might be listening in on their conversation. "Nobody can know where the factory is located. This is an absolute must. They can only know about the marketing office here in Bayport. We have to make sure nothing in the marketing office would lead anyone to the factory or to me for that matter. No addresses. No telephone numbers. No faxes. Nothing."

Henri chuckled as he began catching on to what Peter was subtly suggesting.

Peter continued, "A takeover of DIM Inc. could mean a lot of bad things, Henri. It could mean a shutdown of our operation. Some or all of the personnel could be dismissed. The product would more than likely be altered. The customers would lose their warranties. I'm talking major changes. I'm initiating this strategy plan as much for *your* benefit as I am my own."

"Your right," Henri agreed as he leaned forward with his elbows on the table. "I heard about a company once that lost 90% of its employees as a result of a merger. And the few that got to stay on with the new firm were either demoted or put in departments they weren't familiar with. It was hell for everyone." Henri paused a moment before asking, "Do you want me to memorize pertinent company information?"

"Yes, if you wouldn't mind," said Peter keenly. "That would be better than having a directory somewhere in the office for someone to find. If someone were hell-bent on a takeover they might try anything, including breaking into our office. If we are prepared for this happening we could make sure they found nothing of importance."

Henri became more curious about the strategy plan. "Can't you just say *no* to a merger offer?"

"That's just it, Henri. I've studied many types of mergers. I can't always figure out why a small business owner gives in to the demands. It doesn't seem to be about money. Many of these new hi-tech firms bring in millions of dollars in the first years of business. They are on their way up. So why suddenly sell out at this prime time?"

Henri considered this last remark. "Yes, that is odd, isn't it? Most business owners would only sell their company if it had no future. It doesn't make sense for a prosperous firm to sell out early. Do you suspect some sort of foul play going during these merger meetings?"

Peter did think this was possible. He didn't want to alarm his new marketing manager but takeovers scared him. "Quite possibly," he said a bit tight-lipped. "For me, it is something I don't want to risk finding out." He linked his fingers together. "My only defense, as I see it, is to hide. I realize this sounds ridiculous, but if nobody can find us ... then a merger meeting can't take place either. Can it?"

Henri knew it took a lot of intelligence, planning, time, money, and commitment to launch a new business. To have your hard-earned efforts hi-jacked in the early stages of life did seem rather cruel. A takeover was similar to a kidnapping. The only difference being the victim was a company instead of a child. He thought it was a danger worth guarding against.

"I agree with you," committed Henri. "It's not worth risking.

And besides, it will be a challenge for me to promote the product ... as well as follow through with this strategy plan of yours. I like a challenge."

The two business associates finished their lunch, split the cost of the bill, and headed back to the waterfront office for another marketing session.

*   *   *

It was ten o'clock that night when Peter got back home to Greenvale. He felt pleasantly tired. He used his remote-control device to open the garage door and eased the vehicle inside. After putting the car into Park he shut off the engine.

Peter entered the code in the security panel beside the front door. When the green light came on he pushed the door open and went inside. The heavy door closed behind him with a gentle thud.

It was totally quiet inside the building.

"Tangy!" Peter gave a whistle.

A moment later Tangy came bounding towards him from the direction of the warehouse area.

"How are you doing, boy? Did you miss me?" Peter bent down and gave Tangy a scratch behind his ears. They both headed up to the loft together. Peter plopped his bags down at the top of the staircase and hung up his coat on the coat tree.

The first thing he noticed was the message light blinking on his answering machine.

The first message was from Alex asking Peter when their next meeting was and could they put "security" on the agenda.

The second message was from his real estate agent in Greenvale. "Good news, Peter. We have an offer for your house. Call me when you get this message."

The third message was from Ethel wanting him to check the filing system she had set up in his office. "Was it OK?"

After changing into something comfortable, Peter settled down on the couch to watch the late-evening news.

CHAPTER 21

On October 31st the prototype of DIM was completed. It was an exciting day for everyone at the factory. Each person who had been involved in its development gathered around the new model perched on top of a small workstation in the center of the administrative area.

Peter pulled up an armless swivel chair in front of the test-model. He felt a surge of pride coursing through his veins as he admired the smart-looking machine. *What a beauty!*

DIM was a small all-in-one unit fit together in a singular body with the monitor, hard-drive, and printer all neatly compacted. The edges were curved and smooth giving it a space-age look. The oyster-shell coloring made the computer look dignified and durable. The head of the swivel monitor was tilted back slightly for an improved view.

Alex hooked up a three-prong extension cord and a surge protector to a wall-socket nearby and connected it with the plug of the computer.

Peter snapped on the POWER switch on the right side of the computer. In less than a minute the computer was booted up. Peter studied the opening search screen that came to view. "Nice work, Julie," he complimented the software programmer.

"Now gather around everyone. I'm going to test the prototype to see how well it performs. I have chosen an astronomy-related search for the first test," Peter said to the on-looking design team. "First, I will download my astronomy database onto the hard-drive. Then I will save this database under a new directory called *Astronomy*."

Peter inserted a memory stick into the USB port and began the download process. Then he returned to the opening screen.

"My first search will be to find out any information relating to space explorations that were done in the year 1995. I will enter two keywords: *space travel* and *1995*. I will choose a word-count range of 1,000 words. I will request DIM to search *all* of its directories, including the Astronomy directory." As Peter spoke he typed the words into the appropriate entry lines on the search screen.

"Now I will press the SEARCH key."

Peter tapped a blue key on the right side of the customized keyboard. A moment later a summary screen appeared.

"Wow!" whispered Melanie as she leaned in closer to get a better look.

There were six items listed on page one of the Search Summary. Using the mouse the professor selected the blue underlined title of the first item. A passage of text appeared on the screen. It was an account of a shuttle launching on December 14, 1995, at 15:30 hours, at the *McAllister Space Center*. The passage was an extract taken from an article published by *Space Explorers*.

"Notice how the keywords are highlighted in bold text." Peter pointed out each keyword with his pen as he scrolled down the passage. "Only passages of text that contain *all* the requested keywords, within the specified block range, are chosen. This is important, because it helps narrow the search down to an exact topic. We could, of course, alter the results by changing the keywords or by expanding the text-block range. For now, let's print these results."

Peter pressed the red PRINT button at the left side of the customized keyboard. A few seconds later a sheet of paper slowly inched out of the computer. The paper sliced and fell off into a mounted silver basket.

Everyone clapped and cheered.

Alex snapped up the paper and with a gleam in his eyes said, "Allow me the honor of reading it."

"Be my guest." Peter laughed and folded his arms across his chest while leaning back in his chair.

Alex read the account about the shuttle-launching to the rest of the group. Although they were missing the story's background details they were able to get the general gist of the space mission. After Alex finished reading it everyone cheered.

Peter spun around in his chair and faced the trio. "Now we have our prototype and it works! Congratulations to each of you for the fine work you have done."

"Hey everyone, let's have a party!" Melanie jumped with enthusiasm.

"Yes, definitely," agreed Julie. "This is something worth celebrating."

They agreed on following Tuesday afternoon when everyone could attend. Melanie offered to phone and invite Henri Larue to come down from the Bayport waterfront office for the celebration. Peter offered to pay the expenses. Alex offered to bring in some champagne from his family's private stock. Julie volunteered to do the decorations and arrange for the catering.

For the next couple of hours the team took turns trying out sample searches on the new DIM computer. It proved to be brilliant in all of its functions. It was fast and accurate. It was easy to use. It was a practical genius.

* * *

In the administrative area of the factory, three square tables were covered with white linen tablecloths. In the center of each table was a bouquet of fresh-cut flowers. Surrounding the floral displays were silver trays of canapés, cheese and crackers, pâté, fresh vegetables and dip, and two bottles of champagne chilling in silver ice buckets. Soft strains of music came from the hidden stereo system above.

Most of the guests arrived shortly before one o'clock. Each had dressed for the occasion. Peter wore a taupe-colored suit accessorized by a wide yellow tie. Julie wore a long white dress that fell to her ankles. Alex wore a tuxedo he had found in the back of his closet and had cleaned and pressed for the occasion. Melanie wore a gold two-piece business suit.

Melanie took one of the red carnations from the floral display, broke off the stem, and tucked it neatly in Peter's lapel. "Congratulations, Peter." She leaned up and kissed him on the cheek.

"Thanks, Melanie," Peter beamed.

Henri arrived at 1:15 p.m. with his six-year-old daughter Gigi. He apologized for his wife not being able to attend because she had prior commitments. Gigi stared shyly at everyone with big blue eyes.

The new DIM prototype was sitting on a decorated workstation table with blue and white ribbons streaming down from all sides of the computer. The unit was turned on and the screen-saver showed the word "DIM" flashing on and off intermittently on the screen. The module looked like a tiny spaceship that had recently landed from a faraway galaxy.

Peter Preston began his opening speech to the small group gathered around him. "DIM is a treasure leading to other treasures," he spoke profoundly. "Many great secrets will be discovered from using this portable research computer. To the best of my knowledge there are no other products on the market quite like it. Soon it will be for sale to the general public, businesses, and educational institutions." Peter thanked each person for their contribution in making the DIM prototype.

"Now the business can begin," he spoke crisply. "I hope each of the design team will considering staying on with DIM Inc. to help launch the company. Your work here has already shown itself in many positive ways through this marvelous prototype. To be honest, I never thought it would turn out as good as it has."

Everyone clapped.

Julie stepped forward and handed Peter a gift bag. "We realize you may never be a professor again so we had this made for you." She smiled mischievously and stepped back into the group.

Peter peeked into the gift-bag and pulled out a silver plaque. On the plaque were engraved the words: PETER PRESTON — WORLD'S GREATEST INVENTOR. He began to laugh as he held it up for everyone to see.

Melanie added, "It's meant to go on your office divider."

Peter blushed. "Thank you. You know I do occasionally miss my old job. But I must say ... nothing has given me more satisfaction or pleasure than working on this project. I will proudly keep this plaque. Thanks everyone. Now ... let's celebrate!"

Popping corks and clinking glasses began the celebration party.

"To DIM!" everyone toasted.

* * *

Julie and Melanie gave a demonstration of DIM to Henri and Gigi. Henri was quite impressed. "This really is amazing. Now that I have seen it with my own two eyes, I believe this product will sell."

The party lasted until five that afternoon.

CHAPTER 22

One thousand DIM computers stood neatly in a row. Peter Preston surveyed the first stack of computers in the warehouse storage room. Each box was stamped "DIM" on one side and "Handle With Care" on the other side. *Unassuming,* he thought as he studied them. There was enough image to make the shipment look professional but not too much to draw attention to it. That was OK because it was the product he wanted people to notice and not the company.

Everything had to be ready before the advertising could begin. A stock of products was now on-hand. The ordering system had been setup and tested. The e-commerce website was up-and-running. Customer service was in place. And, last but not least, a success plan had been created.

As strange as it may sound, one of the reasons a new business failed was due to success coming too quickly. If a young business got too many orders, in too short of a space of time — and was not prepared to handle the orders — this could cause a troublesome backlog. The virgin firm would then buckle under the pressure, be unable to delivery the product on time, and end up with a lot of unsatisfied customers. Word would get out that the company was incompetent and the firm's reputation ruined. Once experience was gained, however, and a reserve of cash on hand, then the company

112

could easily handle a large influx of orders. Until this level of maturity was attained, a business owner had to be careful with the number of orders they accepted.

Peter wanted DIM Inc. to succeed as a business but in its own good time. If it took a year or two, that was fine with him. *What's the hurry, if we're making a profit?* he reasoned.

The plan was to do direct-factory sales only. DIM would not be available in retail stores. The reason for this was simple: it would allow them to sell the computers cheaper. Orders would come through the online ordering system and be processed at the Bayport waterfront office before being relayed to the factory in Greenvale.

A manufacturing firm in Bayport had been commissioned to make the parts for the computers. These parts were then sent to DIM's factory, in bulk, to be assembled. The factory would maintain a stock of computers on hand. When the orders increased, the stock would be upped, and a new warehouse would be built. It was a simple development plan.

After doing a final check Peter called Henri and told him to begin the advertising.

*   *   *

It was 8:55 P.M. on a Victoria Day Monday. The scent of pizza filled the Bayport waterfront office. The blinds were closed. All the lights were dimmed except for two wall-mounted brass lamps glowing softly over some inspirational prints in the corners of the reception area.

Peter, Henri, and Melanie were wearing sitting together on the indigo leather sofa drinking rum-punch, eating pizza, and chatting.

They were waiting for the airing of the first infomercial on Channel 22, a regional Shopping Channel.

Henri put a blank DVD into the DVD-recorder and programmed the machine to record the half-hour television commercial. They would be watching the show on a big-screen plasma television they had brought from Greenvale just for the occasion. Later the three would analyze the tape for the infomercial's strengths and weaknesses.

When the infomercial began, Peter immediately noticed the upbeat music in the background. The opening scene began with a scan of an elegant room. There were two potted ferns, a bookshelf filled with books, an easel, a podium, and a workstation table where a DIM model sat waiting in its screen-saver mode. The setting was chic and nicely laid-out.

Alex and Julie walked into the room holding hands. Alex wore a white tuxedo with navy satin lapels. His hair was gelled and groomed back from his face. The cuffs on his shirt glittered with flashes of gold. Julie wore a cream-colored business suit with a short skirt and a turquoise silk blouse. Alex took his place at the podium. Julie took her place at the workstation.

"So far, so good," Peter whispered to the other two on the couch.

Alex began with an introduction of the product. In a clear professional voice he explained what the DIM computers were. He cited several ways the DIM computer could be used in business, education, and in family life. He was charming to watch and the warmth in his voice was compelling to listen to.

Immediately after Alex's introduction, Julie gave several visual demonstrations of the DIM computer. At this point the camera zoomed in for a close-captioned shot allowing the audience to see each step clearly. When the search results were printed, Alex read the passage out loud for the benefit of the invisible audience.

The final portion of the infomercial discussed the price of DIM and ways the product could be ordered. Alex boasted about a special introductory offer which included a bonus of one hundred free databases of popular, useful information. He also discussed the courier delivery option which guaranteed a 3-day shipment.

At the end of the infomercial, streamers and balloons came down from ceiling. Alex and Julie waved good-bye and departed the room. The final shot was of DIM back in its screen-saver mode.

*　　*　　*

As soon as the show was over, Henri jumped up, stopped the DVD, and shut off the TV. "Hey, wasn't that fantastic?" he exclaimed rubbing his hands together. "If that doesn't bring in business, I don't know *what* will."

Melanie, who always had a positive perceptive, said, "The setting was gorgeous. And Alex and Julie looked like a million dollars. I thought the infomercial made the company look sophisticated."

And so DIM made its debut. It was no longer an idea in a dusty folder tucked away in a professor's university files. It was now a real product, one that could be seen, touched, and made to perform feats of intellectual wonder.

CHAPTER 23

A week after the first infomercial aired, almost four thousand orders were placed through the waterfront marketing office. It astounded the management team who had been hoping in the neighborhood of five hundred or so orders. 80% of the orders came via the e-commerce website Peter had set up. What surprised all of them were the six hundred orders from customers requesting their computers to be shipped via courier. Henri thought this was one of the smartest business decisions they had made.

As fast as orders came into the waterfront office, Henri redirected them to the factory to be processed. He was stunned by the steady demand for the new computers. Not being familiar with the world of research, he had been doubtful at first. During the early stages he often wondered if a research computer would even sell at all. Now here he was taking order after order.

Treating each order as if it were prize gold-dust, the personnel of DIM Inc. began the efficient process of assembling and shipping the products to their customers. It was a well-designed system. Everyone worked at an unhurried steady pace. Nothing was allowed to be rushed. No backlog of orders was permitted passed a three-day wait.

Upon receiving another green light from Peter, Henri and Melanie began to work on other advertising plans. A second infomercial was scheduled to be aired the following month, on the same channel, and then each month thereafter for the next ten months, airing at various times of the day.

A newspaper ad was designed and appeared in a selection of national newspapers.

Alex, Julie, and Melanie were invited to stay on with the company for another six months. Peter wanted to make sure the success of the company continued to go smoothly. They each agreed to this arrangement and were assigned a multitude of tasks among them. Because their previous employment contracts had now expired, they dropped their salary and went with the profit-sharing payment only.

*   *   *

DIM was like a new toy. People were buying them just to see all the things they could be used for. It opened up a world of discovery for everyone.

It became obvious to Peter and Henri that an expansion plan would be needed sooner than they had originally thought. Peter set up a special account in the business's accounting system for "expansion" and arranged with the bookkeeper to channel 10% of the company's gross revenue into this account. He set a goal of $1.5 million dollars.

Peter planned to build an additional assembly facility next to the existing factory. He was pleased Lot 66 had so much land. It would allow for more buildings to be quickly erected.

Each of the factory workers was provided with two pairs of

white overalls. Weekly meetings were held to encourage a positive team spirit and to do problem-solving. Problems were discussed with the employees involved in the procedures and their suggestions were valued and often implemented. Peter treated all the workers as an important part of the company.

A reward program was introduced for suggestions that were used in the company. For each idea, the worker received $1000 bonus on their next pay.

It was clear sailing ahead for everyone at DIM Inc. The workers had mastered their jobs. The design team had a new direction to go in. Henri had free reign over marketing the product. Peter was now the boss of a thriving new business.

Could anything possibly go wrong?

CHAPTER 24

"How's everything with you, Alex?" James Wiley casually asked his son from the far end of the dining-room table. It was seven o'clock in the evening and the family was quietly eating dinner together.

Alex was about to take a bite of his sole when his father spoke to him in that quiet-yet-deadly tone of voice he often used when he was broaching an uncomfortable subject. "Oh ... um ... fine, father ... couldn't be better." Alex didn't look up from his plate while he focused on his dinner.

"Humph," responded his father as if he knew differently.

Lately Alex had kept his time spent at the Wiley family home down to an absolute minimum. It was rare he was even home for meals. Most nights he slipped in the back door well passed midnight. He was noticeably reluctant to have conversations with his parents.

James Wiley was an old fox who could glean information out of anyone if he was inclined to. "Things going well with that secret project of yours?" he prodded.

Alex sensed his father knew something about the project but wasn't openly saying it. Alex figured his dad was hoping to trip him up to reveal something. He pushed his chair back a foot away from the table and folded his arms tightly across his chest. *So much for dinner.*

"Extremely well," Alex answered with a confident smile. He

wasn't lying about this. Since the onset of his contractual employment with DIM Inc., he had brushed up on his computer skills, become involved in the development of a new technology, earned himself quite a bit of extra cash, and formed a few lasting friendships with some fine people. On top of this Alex had saved his career from oblivion. He considered this latter achievement to be the ultimate one.

"You're not involved in anything illegal, are you?" persisted his father.

Alex let out an exasperated whoosh of air as though the very idea was ridiculous. He raised his eyebrows at his father and refused to answer.

Irene Wiley quickly interrupted the simmering feud by asking Alex if he was coming to the family barbecue on Saturday afternoon. "Would you like to bring someone, Alex?" she asked.

Immediately Alex thought of Julie Sanders. A smile came to his face as he turned to his mother. He and Julie had been spending some quality time together. He thought she was beautiful and smart. The fact that she never pressured him for a personal relationship made him admire her even more. Maybe she had been stung in a past relationship and now was cautious. He didn't care. He loved being with her.

"Sure mom. I know someone I'd like to ask." Alex was grateful to his mother for her timely intervention.

"Good!" said Irene. "It'll be fun. And bring your bathing suits. We're going to have the pool set up for a game of water volleyball."

Alex finished his dinner quietly. He got up and kissed his mother on the cheek and thanked her for the meal. When he left the dining room he could feel his father's eyes boring tiny holes into his back. Alex left without saying goodbye.

*   *   *

Fifteen miles south of the factory stood a mansion near the river. It had been up for sale for more than five years without much luck of a buyer. Peter drove down the winding driveway covered over with graceful branches of willow trees. He had once known the former owner and remembered attending a party at this house.

The house had been built two hundred years ago by a wealthy "export" merchant. Rumor had it the house was actually used for smuggling goods in and out of Hidden Valley. The house was made of white limestone and the walls were at least eighteen inches thick. It was no wonder it had stood solid after years of weathering storms.

All the well-tended gardens had long gone to weeds. Only a few wildflowers remained blooming faithfully year after year.

It had been a year since DIM Inc. had been in operation and the business was growing rapidly. There was now plenty of money for Peter to invest in new living space. Although the loft quarters in the factory had suited him fine until now, he felt a need for something more spacious and permanent as a home. *Why not spend a bit of my hard-earned profits?*

Peter had noticed the "For Sale" sign at the road entrance while driving from the airport one day. He got out of the Lexus and began nosing around the house looking in windows and inspecting the dwelling's general condition. The windows were too dusty to see through but he managed to glimpse a lonely chandelier hanging in the main living area.

The view of the valley from the back of the house was glorious. He could see for hundreds of miles to the west hills of Hidden Valley. There was a nice flat backyard that would be perfect for installing an in-ground pool. An orchard of neglected fruit trees was planted to one side of the house. A bit of pruning and tree-care would bring them back again.

Peter felt good on the property. He liked the privacy, the view, and the size of the house.

*   *   *

The next morning Peter called the real-estate agent. Two rings later, a pleasant voice said, "Valley Homes. How can I help you?"

"Good morning. My name is Peter Preston. There's a property for sale on Concession Road #5 that is listed with your agency. I know it used to be owned by the Thompson family because I knew them years ago. The agent listed is David Jones. Can you get him to call me about it?"

"Actually Mr. Preston, if you don't mind holding, he's right here in the office."

"Sure, thanks," said Peter.

According to David Jones the house was listed for $250,000 but since it had been vacant for quite awhile David felt sure the owner would come down in price. He offered to give Peter a tour and set a time for the following afternoon.

*   *   *

Peter met David Jones at the house a few minutes after two o'clock the following day. They shook hands and proceeded up a cobblestone path towards the front door. It took David a moment to find the right key from a cluster of keys.

"This house used to be really nice," David said doing his sales pitch. "With a little renovation I bet it could be brought back to its original state."

As the two gentlemen wandered throughout the house David gave Peter a rundown on the property. The living room was four hundred square feet, had a chandelier, maple floors, as well as a working fireplace. The farm-style kitchen had lots of windows. The west side of the house overlooked the river a few hundred yards away. There were four bedrooms on the second floor. Three had their own private bathrooms. The attic was filled with antique furniture, boxes of books, and racks of discarded clothing.

David told Peter one hundred acres of land came with the property. They discussed the possibility of a pool being installed in the garden with a patio surrounding it. "I don't think that would be a problem, Peter. Let me give City Hall a call and see if they would issue a permit for one. It never hurts to find these things out before you buy."

Peter put in a conditional offer of $235,000. David promised to call Peter as soon as he had confirmation from the present owners.

*   *   *

It was seven o'clock the following evening when Peter got a call from David Jones. "They agreed to the offer, Peter. As a matter of fact they seemed awfully glad someone wanted to buy it. You can close the deal whenever you like."

"That's terrific," Peter said. "How about July 20th?"

"Sounds good to me. I'll have the paperwork ready in a couple of days. I'll call you to come in for the signing. Thanks for doing business with Valley Homes, Peter."

"You're welcome." Peter ended the call.

*   *   *

Peter did the renovation plans for the house himself. He made arrangements with the same contractor that had done the work on the factory building to do the work on the house. Renovations were scheduled to begin at the end of August. This gave Peter a chance to arrange for the property to be thoroughly cleaned and exterminated for insects.

As much as Peter liked the size and style of the house he was not one for antiques. He preferred a more contemporary style of decor. So, the chandelier was taken down, the antiques were auctioned off, and the oriental carpets were burned in the backyard. All the floors were carpeted. The wallpaper was removed and painted with a Teflon-coated paint. The wood-burning fireplace was replaced by a gas-lit fireplace; Peter believed it was safer. The moose-head mounted on the wall in the library was removed because it offended Peter's environmental sensitivities. Mounted in its place was a painting of Hidden Valley done by a local artist.

The kitchen was turned into an ultra-modern cuisine center with track lighting, a utensil island, and brand-new electronic appliances. Peter anticipated hosting lots of dinner-parties. *Hey, why not?* He was a successful businessman now.

A thirty-foot pool was installed off the French-door patio. It was heated so it could be used in the winter. Next to the pool was a cedar sauna. One of the bedrooms had been transformed into a fitness room and now had state-of-the-art exercise equipment. After a long day at work there was no better way for Peter to stay in shape.

Tangy adjusted well to the move. He went with Peter in the car to the factory during the day and spent his evenings back at the house. He enjoyed the best of both worlds.

CHAPTER 25

One evening DIM was featured in a product-review television show called *Reviews*. Melanie Gold happened to spot the review while she was surfing channels. As soon as she heard DIM mentioned she quickly recorded the show. She felt sure Peter would want to see it.

Barry Nelson was the host of *Reviews*. He referred to the new computer as "a mystery product" and talked about how the owner and the location of the business were still as yet unknown. Nobody seemed to know why things were being kept a secret. There were many speculations of course. One rumor was the product was actually being sold by *SimTech*, a major technology corporation, who were using the mystery tactic to make sales.

Barry praised the compact features of the computer. He gave a quick overview of the how-to manual. On the negative side Barry claimed that many home-PC users might have little use for the product. In Barry's opinion, the computer was more suitable for use in businesses, educational institutions, and in places like video-stores and libraries.

Melanie interpreted the review as both positive and negative. There was nothing in the show that out-rightly condemned DIM, which was a good sign since the review could help establish DIM as a permanent product on the marketplace. Melanie thought the mystery element might actually help get them more customers because people always had an obsession for secrets.

At the end of the review Barry gave instructions on how to order the new computer. The review lasted twenty minutes.

*   *   *

In spite of Peter's efforts to keep the location of DIM's factory a secret, word did begin to leak out around the working community of Greenvale. Most of the talk pertained to employment opportunities at a new hi-tech facility just outside of town. Employment was not easy to find in the remote region of the valley and, according to rumors, this new company offered high wages and a terrific benefit package. And let's face it, when it comes to money, what type of business is more lucrative than a technology firm?

Nobody made the connection between the assembly plant on Concession Road #5 and the minor sensation of the DIM computers on the marketplace. Only the employees at the plant knew the truth but they had been sworn to secrecy through their signed confidentiality agreements. They weren't about to jeopardize their employment by exposing the mystery through senseless gossip.

The employees of DIM Inc. were permitted to discuss general company information with their family and friends, like salaries and vacations, but they were not allowed to discuss information about the product or who the owner of the company was. This was the basic requirement of the confidentiality agreement. The employees at the factory saw the request in a simpler light. What other company in

127

Greenvale pays $15 an hour as a base rate for unskilled labor? So, they stayed silent.

*   *   *

Late one Friday afternoon, at the end of September, Peter called a general staff meeting at the factory. Chairs were lined up in the administrative area and a podium was set up where Peter would give his little talk. By five o'clock at least seventy-five of the personnel were milling around waiting.

Peter greeted everyone. "I know it's Friday so I'll be as brief as I can. I've called you here to make an important announcement regarding the company. In two weeks ... we are going public! This means, we will be introducing DIM shares for sale at *TechExchange*. This is the stock exchange that buys and sells shares for technology companies. The IPO, or *initial public offering* as it is called, will be $20.52 per share."

The employees clapped at this announcement.

Peter waved his hand and smiled before continuing. "The good news is that each employee of DIM Inc. is permitted to purchase shares in the company at a special rate of $17.30 per share. This will give you voting privileges at stockholder meetings. You will also receive annual dividend payments. Off course you can sell your shares whenever you choose. If you would like to become a shareholder, there is a table by the front door with brochures on how you can go about doing this. Feel free to ask me any questions. I'm available most mornings."

Each personnel took a brochure home with them to study on their own time. They were excited by the news.

* * *

The next morning Peter sat in the observation booth overlooking the assembly area of factory one floor below. He was thinking of ways to free up some of his time. One of his ideas was to promote his Technical Supervisor, George Peppard, to a new position of General Assembly Manager.

George Peppard was a loyal first-rate employee. He had years of hands-on experience and had several technology-related certificates. Some of the other employees called him a "geek" but the truth was George was a hi-tech wizard. He had a natural aptitude for computers. There was almost nothing about computers that George didn't know or couldn't easily find out. He was a walking and talking technology resource.

Peter saw management potential in George the first day he had hired him. Now it was time to put that insight to the test. Pressing the intercom button Peter announced into the speaker, "George Peppard, come to the observation booth."

George looked up from where he was standing and waved up at Peter. He excused himself from a conservation he was having with an assembly worker and jaunted up the stairs two at a time.

"Hello, Mr. Preston. What can I do for you?" asked George in a friendly slightly out-of-breath voice. George was in his early thirties, tall and slim with light-brown dead-straight hair, and wore expensive silver-rimmed glasses. As Technical Supervisor, he handled all of trouble-shooting aspects in the facility.

"Have a seat, George," said Peter indicating a grey cushioned chair in the small booth space. "Would you like some coffee or tea?"

"Sure, tea if it's made," responded George gladly.

When both men were settled Peter proceeded. "George ... I've started plans for building a new assembly facility. It is going to be erected next the existing factory building and ... if all goes well ... it should be completed by the fall. Once we begin production there, I'm going to need a General Assembly Manager. I want *you* to consider accepting this position."

George was taken by surprise. "Me?" he said. "What would the duties involve?"

"You would be overseeing the assembly production, do task delegations, trouble-shooting like you do now, and once a month analyze statistical data. Not all the work would fall on your shoulders though; you would have an assistant to help you."

The offer was intriguing to George. Normally George would shy away from a grand-scale position, but since he knew the ins and outs of DIM Inc. so well, he guessed he could handle the challenge.

"What salary are you offering, Mr. Preston?"

Peter cleared his throat, "The salary starts at 150K ... with four weeks annual vacation ... as well as a few other perks."

George sucked in a quick breath but didn't let on his delight. He discreetly answered, "If you could give me the details about the position in writing, I will consider the offer and let you know my answer by Monday."

"I'll look forward to it," said Peter.

Both men shook hands. George bounded back down the stairs and strode over to his workstation.

*   *   *

Betsy Smith was the bookkeeper for DIM Inc. She was a portly black woman in her mid-forties who always dressed in floral suits. Betsy had attended Greenvale College where she had received a diploma in General Accounting. She was responsible for keeping the company's accounts up-to-date, doing the weekly payroll, and stocking the office-supply center.

Peter nodded to Betsy when he entered the bookkeeping office. He immediately went over to the wall-safe and slid open the paneling. He began to twirl the combination. He did two spins to the left and landed on 36. He did one full spin to the right and landed on the number 12. He did one more spin to the left and went straight to number 9. Peter heard the click of the lock. He pulled down the brass bar and opened the safe.

The inside of the safe was one foot wide by two feet deep. It was chock full of things. On the right were several stacks of cash that was kept on reserve for petty-cash purchases although there was enough money in there to buy a plane-ticket to just about anywhere in the world. At the back of the safe was a metal box full of spare keys. A dozen or so documents were rolled up on the left wall of the safe.

Peter rummaged through the documents until he found the expansion plans for the new assembly plant. He carefully pulled out the roll and tidied the remaining documents. He closed the safe and turned the dial back to zero. He slid the panel back over the safe safely hiding it from view.

Peter tipped the plans toward Betsy as he departed the room.

*   *   *

Upon returning to his desk, Peter noticed a small sealed envelope in his In-basket. He opened the envelope with a silver letter-opener. Inside was a slip of paper with one word written on it: *OK.* Underneath was the signature of George Peppard.

CHAPTER 26

In mid-town Bayport, a prestigious hi-rise building was owned by the city's popular newspaper, *Today's News*.

Susan Sterling was a star journalist for *Today's News*. Her executive office was located on the third floor of the steel-and-glass building. At this particular moment in time, Susan was impatiently tapping her pen against a pad of paper. Tucked in the crook of her shoulder was the receiver of the telephone as she listened to a recorded message on the other end of the line:

Thank you for calling DIM Inc. If you know the extension of the person you are calling, please enter it now. If you wish to place an order, please press 1. If you wish to leave a message, please press 2. DIM is a test product only. We will not be doing any interviews at this time. Please try again in the future.

"Shit!" Susan said and slammed the phone down in annoyance.

She had been assigned the task of interviewing the owner of the company responsible for making the new DIM computers. Like other media representatives, who were also trying to do the same thing, she was running into a dead-end. The search was becoming frustrating.

The recorded message was pleasant enough but it provided no

real leads to follow. *Sure I could leave a message but what was the chance they would respond to it?* Susan rationalized. As soon as the company found out she worked for the press, they were bound to ignore her.

Susan had done a morning's worth of research on the new hi-tech company. So far she had discovered half-a-million computers had been sold, the product had been featured in three reviews shows on television, and everywhere people were talking about DIM. It had adopted the nickname "the mystery product" because no one knew much about the company. This secret had fueled the public's curiosity. And when the public got curious, they wanted more. It was the responsibility of the media to get to the bottom of things.

Susan was determined to be the one journalist who exposed the secret to everyone. Instinctively she knew it would make a great story. And it would be a chance to improve her credentials. *Heck, she might even win an award for the story*, Susan smiled to herself.

Susan's supervisor, Martha Love, had assigned her the task of getting an interview and doing a feature story about DIM Inc. *Easier said than done!* Susan realized as she stared at her scant notes. *Does Martha know how difficult this assignment is proving to be?*

The task was more than difficult; it was weird. Usually new business owners were throwing themselves at the feet of the media, sending out hordes of press releases about their company, practically begging for attention. *So why was this business owner avoiding it?* It made no sense to her at all.

Susan tried the phonebook, her in-house directories, the Internet, and her special contacts at the newspaper, but was still unable to discover the name of the owner or the location of their factory. The only link to the company was an automated 800# for ordering the product and a customer feedback form on a website. *Big deal.* Even their customer service was an automated system and did not allow for person-to-person contact. There seemed to be no way Susan could speak to a person who actually worked for the company. *Maybe they're all androids working there,* she thought facetiously. *Now I'm really losing it.*

Susan Sterling had advanced to her elite position as top journalist because of her superb talent for rooting out a great story. There was no journalistic skill she did not possess or was afraid to use. Some of the other staff members at *Today's News* thought she was a bit ruthless and crossed over boundaries maybe she shouldn't cross. But, on the plus side, they admitted she was effective at her job. When a major story broke, Susan Sterling's name was usually on the bi-line.

Susan suspected something fishy was going on. In fact, this new hi-tech company smelled like the whole Bayport harbor. If she could only solve this darned mystery...

Maybe I need a little help on this one, she grudgingly admitted to herself. She decided to go to Martha Love, her boss and senior editor of *Today's News,* for some advice.

Susan stood up from her desk and straightened her tight-fitting black suit. It was supposed to be a "power suit" but today it wasn't giving her a boost at all. The sexy cloth-confinement just made her feel more aggravated. Throwing the matching jacket over her shoulder with one finger, and swinging her briefcase with her free hand, Susan used her foot to pull the office door closed behind her. Then she headed down the corridor to Martha's office.

*   *   *

All the bosses at *Today's News* had corner offices to give them the best views of mid-town Bayport. It was one of the perks of their high-ranking positions. These offices were larger than the other offices and were decorated with elaborate furnishings.

Susan knocked lightly on Martha's door.

"Come in!" called out a high-pitched female voice from inside.

Susan entered the office and shut the door behind her.

Martha rose from her seat and greeted her. "Hello, Susan. What can I do for you?"

Martha Love was a sophisticated female executive in her early fifties. She had risen in the ranks of power in *Today's News* by being shrewder and smarter than her peers. She still retained a youthful nature. Her jewelry collection was the envy of all the female office staff. Today Martha wore an off-white suit, a green silk blouse, and strand of opals given to her by her first husband.

"Please sit down," Martha said to Susan indicating a blue chair across from her desk.

Susan puffed out her cheeks, blew out a blast of hot air to warn Martha that she was in a bad mood, and plopped down into the chair. She took her notes out of her briefcase and began to relay to Martha the difficulties she had been having tracking down details about the mystery company. She went over the information she had gathered so far.

"Normally Martha, I could easily handle any assignment you give me. But this one has me stumped. I'm running around in circles.

I'm starting to pull my hair out. I've exhausted all of my research possibilities and still have absolutely nothing."

Susan continued in a fluster, "As you probably know, this new DIM computer has become a mild rave. But I can't get a hold of the owners. I couldn't even find out where their factory is located. I was planning an exclusive on this one, but I'm not sure I can even get story at all."

"Really?" Martha suddenly became interested. "Let me see what you have." Martha snapped her fingers and Susan handed Martha the notes. She watched her boss quietly scan the items.

A minute later Susan asked, "Martha, have you ever heard of a business owner imposing a media shut-out, refusing to do interviews?"

Martha laughed derisively. "Noooo... I haven't. Why?"

Susan gave her a brief rundown. "I have tracked down their marketing firm ... it's here in Bayport ... they are handling the promotions. They have been airing an infomercial on Channel 22. I was able to get a phone number but only a pre-recorded message comes on saying that DIM is a test product, no interviews will be done at this time, but please call back in the future. Can you believe it? They are actually refusing to do interviews. What kind of new business wouldn't want free publicity?"

"A test product?" Martha was thinking of something else. "I wonder what they mean by that? You know, Susan, this is probably one of those fly-by-night companies. You know, here today and gone tomorrow. I'm guessing that's why they don't want anyone to know anything about them. They're probably trying to protect their reputation by maintaining a low profile."

"Hmm ... maybe ..." Susan thought about Martha's dismissive suggestion. "Have you ever *seen* one of these new DIM computers?"

"No. I confess I haven't. What's so special about them?" Martha handed the papers back to Susan.

"Yes, Martha, I have. This new computer is a fabulous piece of technology. It can perform unbelievable tasks. It's really quite sophisticated. It is hardly in the same class as hair-growing tonic from some low-class company. If their product is any kind of indicator, these guys are pros. They know what they're doing." Susan leaned back in her chair and fanned the papers over her face as if she were suddenly hot and needed to cool off.

"What would you like *me* to do?" Martha sat down and asked patiently.

"Would you give me some insight on how to track down this mystery company? I want to expose them. I feel more determined than ever to do a story on them, with or without their permission. Please..." Susan batted her eyelashes and gave Martha a pleading look.

"Oh, all right," said Martha, who secretly loved solving mysteries. "Let's set up an appointment ... say tomorrow afternoon around three ... and we'll go over everything you've got together ... in detail. Then we'll plan a way to bring this company out of hiding. How does that sound?"

"Perfect!" Susan jumped out of her chair. If she had any hope of tracking these guys down, it would be under Martha's guidance. Susan gladly agreed to re-schedule her appointments. This project was now a priority. "Thank you, Martha. See you tomorrow at three!"

*   *   *

The Viewing Room was on the eighth floor. All the lights were off except for a small lamp inside the projector. Susan Sterling pushed Play.

"So, what are we watching?" Martha Love asked Susan.

"I was able to obtain a copy of the infomercial that was aired on Channel 22. I thought we could screen it together for any clues about the company."

"Good idea!"

Susan and Martha faced a six-foot screen as they watched the half-hour show. When it came to the part with the credits rolling by Martha suddenly said, "Stop! Go back a bit."

Using the remote control Susan reversed a few frames and then set Play in motion again.

"There!" said Martha excitedly.

Susan paused the show.

Martha got up and pointed to the screen. "You see that name. *Alexander Wiley.* I'll bet you a three-course dinner he's the son of James Wiley, the owner of Wiley Inc. Have you ever heard of the Wileys?"

"No. Who are the Wiley's?"

"They own a chain of office-supply stores," said Martha excitedly. "If Alex Wiley is involved in the DIM computers, then so might Wiley Inc. It's possible the two companies are inter-connected. You know, one sponsoring the other. I want you to do some digging, Susan. Find out as much as you can about Alexander Wiley and Wiley Inc. and see if they are one and the same."

"I'll get right on it." Susan could feel the break she had been waiting for her happening like a dam springing its first leak. "I have a few days off coming to me. I'll use my time off to do some ... *exploring.*" She laughed.

* * *

Upon making inquiries Susan discovered James Wiley was the chief executive officer of Wiley Inc. and did indeed have a son named Alexander who was about thirty years old. *About the same age as the guy in the infomercial,* Susan put two and two together.

The Wiley family estate was located on the outskirts of the city of Greenvale, one hundred and fifty miles east of Bayport.

Susan decided to take a trip to the valley and pay a little visit to the illustrious Wiley's. If she could get an interview with Alex she might discover more about DIM Inc. She packed an overnight bag that included her personal effects, her camera, a recorder, and her wireless laptop computer. She put the bag in the back seat of her SUV Rover. At precisely 5:45 p.m. on Thursday evening she left Bayport and drove eastward along Highway #3.

Heavy clouds were moving in over the evening sky. Occasionally the light from a half-moon could be seen. It was an eerie night. Susan drove quickly but carefully. She wanted to reach Hidden Valley before dark.

The week of frustration was beginning to slip away. She could feel things turning her way. Her journalistic experience taught her to always be in tuned with her senses because it was during these moments that she made most of her discoveries. And now her instincts were telling her she was about to turn over a few stones.

Two hours and thirty minutes later she reached the valley. She kept her eyes peeled for a nice-looking motel with a *Vacancy* sign. As she turned down the main road towards the heart of Greenvale she saw a welcoming neon sign flashing over the Breeze Motel. Putting on her indicator light Susan made a right turn into the motel parking lot.

She parked her SUV in front of the motel office and went inside. The front desk area was paneled in wood and the decor was old-fashioned but clean. An elderly man of about seventy years of age greeted her. "Are you looking for a room for the night?" he smiled at Susan.

"Yes," replied Susan. "Actually, could you make it for *two* nights. I want to do some site-seeing while I'm here in the valley. What do you have in the way of vacancies?"

"Let me see." The clerk checked through the guest-registration book pretending they were booked up but in fact there were several occupancies. "I've got a second-floor room with a great view for $79 a night. How does that sound?"

"Sounds fine," said Susan, "Where do I sign?"

She filled out a guest card, made her payment for two nights, and bought a map of the local area. Susan got back in her SUV and drove directly underneath the balcony where her room was located. Taking out her overnight bag she locked up the car and climbed up the stairs to Room 221.

The room was spotlessly clean. All the furnishings were new. Susan locked the door and headed straight for the shower. Two hours on the road had left her feeling gritty.

After she had freshened up she found a phone book and ordered some take-out fish-and-chips to be delivered to her room at the motel. When the food arrived, Susan settled at the head of the queen-size bed, with a couple of pillows behind her back, and began to eat and watch a movie.

*   *   *

Susan woke the next morning at 8:00 to the tiny beeping of the electronic alarm on her watch. She quickly dressed, got into her SUV, and drove to the nearest coffee. Going through the drive-thru lane she placed her order.

Using the map she had purchased the night before, she drove to Eagle Road and headed south. When she reached Valleyview Drive she made a right-hand turn. She began to watch for signs of the Wiley estate on either side of the road. Soon Susan found a mailbox at the end of a driveway that said WILEY.

A six-foot black wrought-iron gate barred the entranceway. It was locked. She got out of the car and studied the gate. It had a security system. Susan guessed the gate would only open from the main house or from a remote-control device inside of one of the Wiley's cars.

On both sides of the gate were eight-foot cedar hedges that provided the estate with the ultimate in natural privacy. It would be impossible to climb over them and they were too dense to push through. There was no way she could get inside unless she buzzed to get in. *What would I say?* It seemed too much to explain over an intercom.

Susan decided to park her SUV inside a small driveway just down the road from the Wiley estate entranceway. From this concealed spot, nobody could see her unless they deliberately looked in, however, she could see the entrance to the Wiley estate perfectly clearly. *Now for the wait*

Susan munched on a whole-grain bagel and sipped her latte while she watched the gate. Shortly after nine o'clock the Wiley gate slowly opened. Susan perked up. She set down her coffee cup in the cup-holder of the console. A long gray continental car with darkened windows drove out and headed north — in the opposite direction of where Susan's car was parked. She guessed it was probably Wiley Sr., or his wife, since she couldn't imagine young Alex Wiley driving that style of a car.

She continued to wait.

Twenty minutes later the gate opened again. This time a silver convertible came out and headed in her direction. It sped by so fast Susan was unable to get a clear view of the driver. Her instincts told her this must be Alexander Wiley.

Susan started the SUV and began to follow the silver car. She had to step on the gas to keep up. Susan could see the taillights of the silver car as it braked over the crest of a hill. Her heart was racing inside her. She had never driven this fast before. It was a bit unnerving. *I hope I don't lose him.*

Susan gripped the wheel tightly and pursued with the chase. After ten minutes of hair-raising road-spin, the silver car suddenly vanished from sight. When Susan came to the spot where the car disappeared, she stopped.

"Where the hell am I?" she whispered as the SUV bumped its way down a pebbled road and across a wooden bridge.

Susan's eye caught the flash of something darting across the road in front of her. "What was that?" she said breathlessly. *Geez, everything is making me nervous.* As she drove by, she saw a Siamese cat perched on top of a moss-covered stone glaring at her.

Susan's heart was beating fast. When she emerged into a clearing she slammed on the brakes. Susan was amazed to see a parking lot with about twenty vehicles. The silver car was pulling into a vacant spot. Susan watched as a dark-haired man climbed out of the car, shut the door, and head towards an old brick building. Susan glanced up at a sign over the front door that said: RESEARCH TECHNOLOGY EQUIPMENT.

"Gottcha!" Susan whispered out loud. She put the SUV in Park not daring to go any further because she didn't want to be seen. *No wonder nobody could find the place.*

Using her Nikon zoom-lens camera, Susan began to take a series of photos. She flashed the building, the parking lot, and a picture of Alex's car showing a clear shot of his license plate. With her notebook and pen, Susan recorded all the details of her discovery.

She felt as pleased as punch. One part of the secret was now exposed — the location of the factory! This discovery was going to add another notch in her journalistic tree of success stories.

Backing out to the concession road, Susan made her way to the Breeze Motel.

CHAPTER 27

Peter got a call on his cell phone from Henri Larue in Bayport. "Peter, can you pick up a copy of *Today's News* in Greenvale?"

"Sure," answered Peter. "Why? What's up?"

Henri hesitated a moment. "I don't want to discuss it over the phone. Log on for an online chat after you read the paper. You'll know what I mean by then."

"OK. Give me a couple of hours. I'll go online at say ... two o'clock."

Peter experienced a faint qualm of fear as he disconnected his cell phone and reached for his jacket. *What was in the newspaper he needed to know about?* Maybe it was a bad review.

Ten minutes later Peter parked his car in front the Greenmart on the edge of Greenvale and bought a copy of *Today's News*. He tossed the paper onto the passenger seat and drove back home.

Back in his sunny kitchen, Peter made a second cup of coffee and began to scan the newspaper for any article Henri might want him to read. *What could it be?*

Sure enough on page five of the Business section, at the bottom-right hand corner, Peter found the offending article, along with a photograph he immediately recognized. It was a picture of the factory building. The article read:

DIM FACTORY FOUND

By Susan Sterling, Today's News Staff Write

On Friday, June 21, a reporter from Today's News discovered the location of the factory that makes the popular new DIM computers. Until this time the location of the factory had remained a mystery. The factory was discovered off Concession Road #5, five miles southeast of Greenvale, a small city in the heart of Hidden Valley, 150 miles east of Bayport. The factory is operating inside a renovated century-old brick building. All attempts by the journalist to contact the owners have still failed. A possible link between Alexander Wiley, son of industrial magnate James Wiley, CEO of Wiley Industries, and DIM Inc. is suspected. Alex Wiley was featured in a recent infomercial promoting the new computers and who, coincidentally, resides within a few miles of the factory. Alex was seen entering the factory on June 21. Today's News attempted to obtain an interview with Alex Wiley to see if he could provide more information about the "mystery product" and its owner(s). According to Ian Sullivan, public relations officer of Wiley Industries, Alex Wiley is currently on vacation and will be unavailable for the next few weeks.

*   *   *

Peter logged on for an online chat with Henri using his wireless laptop. He started the communication.

PETER: "Hi Henri. I read the article. I see what you mean.

Do you think it spells trouble?"

HENRI: "You bet I do. Someone has obviously been monitoring us. Not that I am surprised. I expected it to happen eventually."

PETER: "So did I actually. It'll probably be a roller-coaster ride from here on in, don't you think? The press will soon figure everything out, now that they have gotten this far."

HENRI: "Is there any chance of you coming in to Bayport to discuss this? I could pick you up at the train station on Friday at say 11 a.m."

PETER: "You can count on it. See you then."

They both logged off.

* * *

Henri and Peter weren't the only ones who had read the article in *Today's News*. James Wiley also stumbled across the article while having his morning toast. At first it meant nothing to him. But when he got down to the part that mentioned his name, he went into a mild state of shock. James re-read the article two more times before the meaning of it slowly penetrated the numbness of his mind.

He was outraged. *How dare they link my company with this one?* He began muttering angry expletives under his breath. This caught the attention of his wife, Irene, who was quietly planning her day at the other end of the breakfast table. "What is it, James? Why are you getting so upset?" Irene asked her irritated husband.

James read the article out loud for the benefit of Irene.

"Don't you see, Irene," seethed James Wiley. "This is that secret project Alex has been working on ... the one he has so carefully avoided telling us about. And now ... here is this article about the company in the paper ... and it is linked to *me*!" He was shouting by now. "How is this going to look for Wiley Industries?" James shook the paper hard as though he were trying to physically dislodge the offending article from it.

"Honestly, James, if you don't calm yourself down you're going to have a heart attack," Irene scolded her red-faced husband.

James ignored her concern. "I'll bet you a million dollars, Irene, this thing is going to bring us trouble — with a capital T!"

"I don't believe that. You know Alex would never do anything to bring scandal to the business or to our family. He is a mature, responsible young man. I really don't understand why you're so upset. So what if Wiley Industries is mentioned in a newspaper article. Those DIM computers are popular. It'll probably bring in more business for us."

"Humph," snorted James, not believing her. "When Alex gets back from his trip in the mountains, I'm going to have a talk with him!" He shook the paper again and went back to reading.

CHAPTER 28

Henri cut out the article from *Today's News* and made a photocopy of it. He wanted to study it for clues on what might be the result of the exposure.

When Peter arrived at the waterfront office on Friday morning, they got right down to business. "What's your take on this article, Henri?"

"It seems both good and bad to me. For the good, the article makes our company look interesting when it refers to the "mystery" part. For the bad, whoever is behind this investigation is obviously determined to find out everything they can about us. You can be sure they eventually will."

"You are right, Henri. If they figured out where the factory is, it is only a matter of time before they find out who owns the building. A hundred-dollar bill at the Planner's Office in Greenvale might loosen up that fact. I wonder what their next move will be?"

Henri shook his head. "Who knows? But we need to figure out if this exposure will have any negative repercussions. We've been in business for a couple of years now. We're doing pretty well too. Isn't that what you said in the beginning: *that once we're successful enough we can put up a better fight.* Maybe we *are* ready for some media attention now."

Henri felt certain DIM Inc. could hold up in a corporate battle if things came down to that. What he wasn't sure about was the type of fight they might end up getting into. Maybe there was nothing to worry about.

Peter said, "This Susan Sterling from *Today's News* must have followed Alex to the factory. How else could she have found the place? That's a bit devious, don't you think ... but I guess it's typical of the tactics journalists use."

Henri agreed. "In my experience there is *nothing* a journalist won't do to get a story. It's what they do for a living. When you run up against people who are ruthless, or who use underhanded techniques, you know you are in a different ball game. It can put you at a disadvantage ... especially when you're an honest Joe."

Peter mildly wondered what James Wiley thought of all of this. He knew from conversations with Alex his father hadn't been all that keen about his son working for DIM Inc. Seeing an article like this one was bound to make things seem more suspicious.

Henri pointed out a positive side. "This article might bring in more business. Once people know we're legitimate, the sales should increase."

"Yes ... but at what cost in the long run? Now other companies are going to find out facts about our company. Some CEO may want to get friendly with us. I don't like it Henri. I don't think I'm ready for the kind of high-handed business dealings some corporate people get into. I like things the way they are."

Henri was aware of the pressure tactics some corporate owners used against smaller business owners to make them more cooperative.

"Make sure you screen all your calls. Keep alert for anything unusual. What else can you do?"

"Probably not much. Henri, have you ever been involved in any kind of corporate crime ... willing or not?"

Henri mulled through his memories. "The closest I got to something serious was with a case of fraud. A guy I worked for was being investigated by the government for six million dollars that suddenly appeared in his business bank account. He tried to pass it off as a legitimate business transaction but the authorities wouldn't buy it. They pestered him for months. They wanted receipts and answers and anything they could use to piece the puzzle together. In the end they let him go — insufficient evidence. Still, while it was happening, it was nerve-wracking on everyone who worked for the company. None of us knew from one day to the next if it would be our last day of work."

"Sounds like it was a tense time." Peter could feel a tension building in the air now due to this new development. It was more like a sense of something not being quite right. *What was it? What was he missing?*

"What shall we do now?" asked Henri.

"How about a drink? We could both use a little something to get our minds off this."

"Sounds good to me." The two men closed up the waterfront office and headed downtown to the *Starlight* lounge.

CHAPTER 29

The *Secret Hideaway* was a resort nestled in the mountains north of Hidden Valley. It was built from cedar trees and hand-cut stones. Positioned on a rocky ridge the lodge provided premium views of the expanse of the valley below. From morning until night the view changed as light altered the valley's appearance.

There were twenty-four self-contained units in the resort each with its own terrace. The inside of the units were decorated in warm colors of beige and amber. Each had a king-size bed covered with a gold-colored duvet stuffed with goose-down. A stone fireplace was fully stocked with hardwood for a fire that would take away the chill of the nighttime air.

Most of the resort's clientele were couples seeking a little privacy in their lives. One guest was a writer and another was an outdoor artist painting some of the surrounding exotic scenery.

Alex Wiley and Julie Sanders were booked in Unit #10. They had been at the resort for three days now and were planning to stay for two more days. At the moment the couple was soaking in a natural hot-springs pool in a cliff a quarter of a mile above the resort. Enormous rocks and shrubs surrounded the pool of warm water offering the ultimate in private bathing. Alex and Julie were the only guests in the pool.

Alex was telling Julie about his situation in the Wiley family business. "I know it is customary for the first-born son to inherit the family business," he said to Julie who sat across the pool facing him. "Personally, I'd rather do something else with my life. Office supplies are just not my thing. Dad is a real control-freak too. He rules the business like a medieval monarch. Nobody is allowed to make their own decisions. He never lets anyone do what they want."

Julie swirled her arms around her making ripples in the water. She was completely naked. Leaning her face forward she blew a few bubbles in the water. "Is there anyone else in your family that could take over the business ... when your father retires?"

Alex inched a little closer to her. "Yes. There's my sister Katherine. She's actually the one who loves Wiley Industries. She is a lot more devoted to it than I am. But Dad doesn't notice it ... much less appreciate it. My guess is it's because she is female. He's a bit of a chauvinist, in my opinion. I'm not, by the way." He chuckled, pleased with himself.

Julie smiled. "That's good to hear." She leaned closer and kissed Alex on his wet shoulder. "Maybe you should encourage her to take charge. Tell her what your plans are. Then you could be free to do whatever you want. She could be the new Wiley boss. It's the perfect solution."

Alex noticed her nose was getting sunburned and there were more freckles on her face than a week ago. "That's easy for you to say. You don't have a tyrant for a dad. Try convincing *King of the Old School* to let go of the reins."

Julie understood where Alex was coming from. She had

learned early in life to make her own choices and to live with the consequences. "Keep doing what you're doing. Eventually your dad will get used to it. After all, it's *your* life, isn't it? I think you're doing some terrific things. Take the DIM project, for example. What could be better than working on that?"

Alex reached over and pulled Julie backwards into his arms. "You're right. It's the best job I've ever had." He pulled her close to him while he leaned back against a boulder behind him. Now they were both facing the view together. Julie rested her head against Alex's shoulder totally relaxed and utterly happy.

"Thanks for your confidence in me," Alex whispered in her ear.

CHAPTER 30

Oroton began as a gold-mine settlement two hundred years ago. The gold was first discovered by the Oro brothers who had traveled to the site using a treasure map. The mine was established under their family name: *Oro Gold Mine*. Although the gold was now depleted, the name continued on as a legacy to the town's founders.

Situated on the edge of the Cactus Desert, Oroton thrived like an oasis. In its present day it was a sprawling city with one million citizens. Since there were no natural boundaries to keep the city compact, it grew out in all directions.

Oroton was famous for one unusual phenomenon. There were more millionaires per capita in Oroton than in any other city in the country. To some this was a curious fact. Since the gold was gone, where did all the money come from?

The answer was simple: *Dick Drekkel.*

Dick Drekkel began his career fifteen years ago in Oroton as a financial planner. He had a brilliant mathematical mind. He used this aptitude for a worthwhile cause: *analyzing stock reports.* Drekkel would study patterns in the stock market, draw up charts, form conclusions about which stock should be bought and which should be sold, and then post his findings on a bulletin board in his basement office on Brand Street.

When Drekkel was only eighteen years old he made his first

serious investment in the stock market. His insight proved to be very valuable. By the time he was twenty-one Drekkel had amassed twenty million dollars as a result of his ingenious stock decisions. He knew when and what to buy and he knew when and what to sell. His earnings poured into his business, Drekkel Corporation.

Drekkel used a secret formula. He would study trends affecting businesses and communities and then chose companies that made products or services that satisfied those trends in some way. For example, when everyone got into the fitness trend, Drekkel invested in stock from companies that sold fitness-related products or services. He looked for growth potential in those companies and then used this information as a benefit for his clients. He then advised them on what stocks to buy and which ones to sell, for a healthy commission, of course.

One by one each of his clients became rich too. All thanks to Dick Drekkel. When he said "buy" they bought. When he said "sell" they sold. And now their bank accounts were bursting at the seams because of his timely wisdom.

It wasn't long before Drekkel became famous, or "infamous" as some skeptics said, for making millionaires out of the citizens of Oroton. Now there were hundreds of social-climbers scaling the walls of this desert city, all of them rich because of the clever tips provided by Dick Drekkel.

But Drekkel wasn't satisfied with this "minor" success, as he modestly put it. He wanted more. So he branched out into the world of online marketing and began specializing in Internet-based promotions. Soon he was making a million dollars every day in a pay-per-click advertising company called *PaperClick*, a subsidiary firm of Drekkel Corporation. These profits added to the coffers of its parent company like streams channeling into a main river.

Dick Drekkel was proud of himself. Who wouldn't be? He had graduated from Oroton Community College with an A+ in Economics. He had developed a skill in stock analysis that was unique and effective. And now, at the ripe age of thirty-four, he was running an international company that brought in more money than all the other patrons of the Bank of Oroton put together.

Drekkel was a bachelor. He had auburn hair, emerald-green eyes, and a wicked temper. He was all smiles when things were going his way. But when things went wrong, he was like a solar flare with a UV personality. Drekkel became downright dangerous when he got mad. Most of his business acquaintances had learned that first-hand. If they did something that he didn't like, they soon heard about it. Now many of them took extra precautions not to blow any of Drekkel's fuses.

Drekkel was well aware that it was *his* insight that had made his clients rich. He assumed each of them would be eternally grateful to him for the boost he gave them in their lives. And most of his clients, in fact, were appreciative. Those who weren't soon found themselves back in the 24K salary bracket.

The present-day head office for Drekkel Corporation was located in the south end of Oroton in a posh building situated on a lovely landscaped lot. A view of the Oro River could be seen from the west side of the building. All the executive offices were on the penthouse floor.

Every morning Drekkel took a trek around the penthouse corridor, dropping in unexpectedly on any employee he chose. He knew this unnerved them. *But hey, that's what keeps the workers on their toes.*

Veronica Hill was the head receptionist of the penthouse floor. She was twenty-nine years old and had worked for the firm for ten years. She had long black hair, was tall, and wore elegant office attire. She had an assistant typist working under her watchful eye. Veronica was known around the office for someone who got things done.

She secretly adored her boss. She thought if there was a money god it would have to be Dick Drekkel. After all, wasn't that the reason his eyes were green?

When Veronica arrived at work, shortly before nine, she peeked in on her boss before going to her desk. Today, she found Drekkel sitting at a workstation in the far corner of his office huddled over the keyboard of a computer. Veronica quietly snuck up behind him.

She peeked over his shoulder and could see it was one of the new DIM computers he had ordered a couple of weeks ago. He said he planned to use it for doing stock research. Veronica leaned over his shoulder. "What are you working on?" she whispered softly in his left ear.

Drekkel jumped in his chair as though he had been caught viewing a porn site. He shook his mane of hair and gave a little laugh. "Oh hi, Veronica, you startled me." He quickly regained his composure. "You should try this computer. It isn't like any other computer you've ever seen. It's an amazing digital library. It can give you facts on anything and everything."

Veronica set her purse down beside the chair next to her boss. "I've seen a review about this computer on television but I've never actually seen one before. They had some pretty positive things to say about it. Show me how it works."

Veronica retrieved a stool from across the office and placed it next to Drekkel's chair. For the next twenty minutes, Drekkel demonstrated the DIM computer by performing a few searches relating to the stock market.

"That's fabulous!" Veronica drawled in her natural southern accent as she watched the results being printed out of the side of the computer. She glanced over the results on the paper. "What a super little machine!"

Veronica wasn't the only person impressed with the new computer. Drekkel found it impressive too. "Do me a favor, will you, Veronica," he said to her. "See if you can find out what company makes these computers. Who owns it? That sort of thing. I think I'd like to buy some stock in this company, if they're listed."

"Sure, I can do that," responded Veronica as she jumped up from her stool. "It'll give me an excuse to put off doing the quarterly reports." She gave her boss a smile.

"Oh no, you don't. Those reports have to be done by the end of this week ... the annual meeting is on Monday night ... if I don't have those reports..."

Veronica laughed and gave him a small punch in the shoulder. "I'm just teasing. I'll have them done this afternoon."

Veronica picked up her bag and pranced out of the office and headed towards the central lobby where the reception area was located.

She stored her purse under the desk and began to prepare for the day.

* * *

That afternoon Veronica began to tackle the research assignment her boss had given her. She went to the website of her favorite search engine. In the search bar she quickly typed in three letters: D I M. Clicking on the Search button, she waited for the results to appear.

Veronica frequently used search-engines on the Internet. She had a knack for acquiring relevant information on just about any topic. Research was one of her many duties at Drekkel Corporation. Many of the managers requested her assistance in research projects.

Veronica browsed down the first page of results looking for items that might be relevant to the new DIM computer. She discovered an article written by a journalist named Susan Sterling. The article had been published four months ago, in Today's News, a newspaper operating out of Bayport. "I'll bet *she* knows more about this company," Veronica said to herself. She jotted the information on a steno pad.

A quick call to the telephone directory gave Veronica the phone number for the newspaper's office. She tapped in the long-distance number using the rubber end of her pencil. Three rings later, a brisk male voice answered, "Good morning, Today's News, how may I help you?"

Veronica answered in an equally brisk voice. "Could you connect me to Susan Sterling, please. I'm calling from Drekkel Corporation in Oroton."

"One moment, please."

After thirty seconds of jazz music in the background, Susan came on the line. "Susan Sterling."

"Hello. My name is Veronica Hill. I'm calling on behalf of Dick Drekkel ... of Drekkel Corporation ... in Oroton." Veronica knew from previous experience the casual mention of her boss's name often brought her more prompt service, since he was so well known. "Mr. Drekkel has asked me to find out about the company that makes the new DIM computers. I noticed from an Internet search that you have recently published an article about this company. Would you be willing to meet with Mr. Drekkel to tell him what you know about this firm?"

Susan considered the request for a moment before answering. "It isn't much, I'm afraid. But yes I would be happy to meet with Mr. Drekkel. It would have to be here in my office in Bayport though. Would that be OK?"

"Yes. I'm sure it would." Veronica decided to jump on the opportunity and agree to it on her boss's behalf. "He's planning a business trip there next week. Can I call you back for an appointment time?"

"Sure," said Susan smoothly. "I'll be here until five."

*   *   *

Whenever Veronica got a chance to please her boss she went for it with gusto. It had become a secret pleasure of hers to find ways of making Drekkel happy. This was no easy task, mind you. Drekkel was sometimes impossible to please.

Veronica buzzed him from the intercom at the reception desk. "Do you have a minute?" she asked.

"Sure. But could you make it quick? I'm on my way to a meeting."

Veronica went down to Drekkel's office and knocked lightly before slipping inside. It was OK to do this, since he was expecting her.

"Good news." Veronica wore a smile as she approached his desk. "I have a lead from someone who can give you info on the company that makes the DIM computers."

"Hey that's terrific, Veronica." Drekkel was genuinely pleased. He leaned back in his chair and linked his fingers together behind his head. "Who is it?"

"It's a journalist who works for Today's News ... a newspaper office in Bayport. Her name is Susan Sterling. She recently wrote an article about the company. She has agreed to an interview with you ... but it has to be in her office. She won't come here."

"That's OK." Drekkel reached over and began thumbing through his daily planner. "I have a meeting in Bayport next Tuesday. Set up an appointment with her in the afternoon, will you."

This was exactly what Veronica hoped her boss would say. She gave him a big smile. "Will do!"

CHAPTER 31

On the following Tuesday afternoon, at precisely 4:00 o'clock, Dick Drekkel knocked three times on Susan Sterling's office door.

Susan quickly snapped her compact closed and tossed it in her handbag. She was glad she had time to fix her lipstick. She went to the door and opened it.

The towering figure of Dick Drekkel came through her door like a breeze in from the furnace room. Susan almost fell over at the sight of him. He was a powerful figure. Suave. Sophisticated. Someone in complete command of himself.

Drekkel glanced around the office briefly, as though he were making an inspection, before approaching Susan with an outstretched hand. "So good of you to give me a few moments of your time, Ms. Sterling," Drekkel spoke in a tenor tone. He gave her hand a firm shake.

"Please have a seat, Mr. Drekkel," Susan pointed to a chair on the other side of her desk. For some reason, she suddenly felt nervous of her visitor. "I'm afraid I don't have a lot of time. I'm catching a flight this evening. How can I help you?"

Susan felt self-conscious in her short skirt as she sat down. *Who is this man?* Susan mildly wondered as she gazed at his handsome face. He looked rich. He looked famous. He looked like he was used to getting his own way.

"I want you to tell me *anything* you can about the company that makes the DIM computers." Dick touched his fingertips together in a tee-pee. *And don't bother trying to refuse me,* was what he didn't say but meant. "I'm considering making an investment in their firm and need a little background information before I do."

"Yes, of course. I took out my file for you. I'm afraid there isn't much information to give you. I had a hell of a time getting even this much. But there are some photos you might like to see."

Drekkel's eyebrows shot up. *Photos?* Susan handed them to him. There were three 8 X 10 photographs of what appeared to be pictures of the outside of a factory building. He stared at the photos in wonder.

Susan could see the puzzled look on Drekkel's face. "I'll give you two guesses what those photos are," she said with a chuckle.

Drekkel smiled. "Their factory, right?"

Susan burst out laughing. "Yes! Can you believe it? That building had to be a hundred years old if it was a day. It had obviously been fixed up in a hurry. It is where they assemble the product. I discovered the building in a remote area near Greenvale. Isn't it a hoot?"

165

Drekkel looked at the photos again. A slow smile began to spread over his face. Even though he was too polite to agree with the journalist, he had to admit to himself the building did seem a tad shabby. "Did you meet the owner?"

"No. I wasn't able to find anything out about the owner. They have a marketing office here in Bayport though. Down on the waterfront. *That* office is quite nice. It isn't anything like the factory. I wrote the address down somewhere. Here, let me find it for you."

Susan sorted through the items in the folder to find the address. When she did, she copied it down on a pad of paper and handed the slip to Drekkel.

Drekkel took the note and put it in his jacket pocket. Looking at the photos one more time, he said to Susan, "Doesn't seem to be very elaborate, does it? But they're new. They'll probably expand in time. Do you know anything else about them?"

"The only other thing I learned is that these computers are becoming *very* popular. They are receiving some rave reviews. I heard through the office grapevine, they have already sold a million computers. Considering their modest facility, I would say, that's a pretty good effort."

Susan told Drekkel she wasn't sure if the trend would last. As a journalist she had witnessed many pop companies come and go quickly. DIM Inc. might just be another blip on the business screen.

"I would be very interested in anything else that you might learn about this company. Here's my card." Drekkel pulled out a business card from a gold case and deftly handed it to her between two fingers.

"Can I ask why you are so interested in this company, Mr. Drekkel?" Susan was a conscientious reporter who always wanted to know more.

"Like I said, I'm planning to invest in the company ... that's all I can say right now." Drekkel gave her a phony smile. *You don't need to know anything else.*

Drekkel stood up. "Thanks for your help, Ms. Sterling. Have a nice day." Quietly he departed the office.

*   *   *

Susan Sterling sat at her desk staring at the wall for a good five minutes after Drekkel left. When she came out of her trance, she began to put the items back into the folder. It was then she noticed that the photos were missing. *Did Drekkel take them? I wonder why?*

*   *   *

Drekkel returned to Oroton the next morning. He arranged a meeting with his stockbroker, Bill Crane, at the Boneyard Café on Sandy Boulevard. It was a warm evening in spite of it being early October. The two longtime friends sat at a corner table on the outdoor patio. The deck jutted out by the rushing waters of the Oro River. Some of the spray from the water made a fine mist in the air.

Drekkel ordered a locally-made beer. Bill Crane ordered a vodka stinger. They shared a bowl of honey-coated cashews between them.

"Bill, I want you to buy some shares for me ... in a company called DIM Inc. They are listed at TechExchange. But I don't want anyone to link me to the shares ... at least not for now."

Bill looked amused. "Oh? Do tell me more!" He had known Dick Drekkel since their days in college together. They had attended many of the same classes and the two were frequently involved in schemes.

Drekkel slid a sealed envelope across the table towards Bill. "There are five corporate names in this envelope. Set up separate brokerage accounts under each of these five names. Then buy stock from DIM Inc. and distribute the shares amongst these five accounts. Keep buying shares a little at a time over the next few months. Do it until you have *almost* 5% of their total company shares in each of the five accounts. But don't go as high as 5% though. Go only as high as ... say ... 4.8%."

Bill was used to unusual requests from Drekkel. He put the envelope in the inside pocket of his jacket and chuckled. "What are you planning to do, Dick? ... take over the company?" he asked in jest.

"As a matter of fact, I am," Drekkel smiled and raised his glass. "Cheers!"

CHAPTER 32

Peter, Alex, and Julie sat around the boardroom table discussing ideas for the next version of DIM.

Julie said, "I have been working on a new feature of DIM that would allow a user to perform an *online* search and save the results. This new feature would allow the operator to do a search using a search-engine ... and then perform a second *DIM search* on these results. It is sort of a double-search process.

"To include this feature, a web-browser will need to be incorporated into DIM's software. I am in the process of getting permission from a software company to use one of their web-browsers. When that comes through, we can proceed with this new feature.

Julie continued, "I still have a few quirks to work out. Once this new feature is developed, it would mean a user could use a DIM computer to do online searches, as well as searching the main databases on the hard-drive."

"That's terrific, Julie." Peter was the most impressed. "Online searches! What a great idea. If we branch into the online world we can really expand our customer base. If you are able to include this new feature, it would make DIM a more competitive product."

"Exactly!" Julie agreed. "The problem with existing search-engines is they tend to bring in too many results. It is not uncommon for a set of keywords to produce thousands, even millions, of results. This makes search-engines time-consuming. People want their information quickly and concisely. They don't want to spend an hour wading through websites to find what they want.

She explained, "The search process in DIM is much more exact than a search-engine. By fine-tuning the search-engine's results with a second DIM search, you could cut back on the number of results. Plus, you can *save* the results in a directory on the DIM computer ... for future reference. No search-engine allows the operator to save the results."

Peter mused, "DIM might become a better way to use the Internet than a PC with a web-browser."

Alex admitted he used his PC for the surfing the Internet at least 75% of the time. This included doing web-based email. The only other times he used his PC were for typing the occasional letter to someone. "If we can make this work, people might even abandon their PC's and go with a DIM computer only."

"How long do you think it will take you to finish programming this new feature, Julie?" Peter asked. He knew this new development would improve his business's chance of competing in the industry.

Being able to advance within the field would guarantee continued success.

"Maybe a month ... maybe less," Julie replied optimistically. "I have the preliminary work done already. There are only a couple of *minor* quirks. Perhaps Alex could assist me in helping solve these?"

Alex readily agreed.

For the sad news, Peter informed the team that Melanie Gold would no longer be working for DIM Inc. She had opened a new office in downtown Greenvale to better serve her clients of Gold Advertising. Everyone was invited to attend the grand opening on Friday afternoon.

Henri Larue would now be handling all marketing and promotions out of the waterfront office in Bayport.

* * *

Production at the factory had reached its maximum. There were now two assembly shifts: day and evening. A new assembly facility was in the process of being built adjacent to the existing factory building.

All orders were direct-factory sales. Peter found this to be an ideal method. It required no sales personnel because there was no retail middleman. Many of the customers chose to pay extra for courier delivery. They liked getting their DIM computers pronto. This was proving to be a bonus for business too, not just for DIM Inc., but also for Valley Courier, a local courier service operating out of Greenvale.

The "replacement policy" turned out to be a wise decision. Instead of training repairpersons to do repairs, faulty computers were simply replaced and the bad units disassembled. It was a fast and cheap way of dealing with this occasional problem. Peter was pleased it didn't actually happen that often. He felt proud that his DIM computers were so well made they almost never broke down.

Peter believed one of the reasons why the DIM computers rarely broke down was because no external software programs were permitted on the hard-drives. This was typically where viruses came from in regular PCs. Foreign software programs sometimes were infested with worms or viruses. On the DIM computers, only data was permitted to be saved on the hard-drive; data was generally 99% virus-free.

Peter treated every one of his customers with respect. Each got one-on-one service. Peter knew even one unsatisfied customer (with a loud voice) could damage the reputation of his business permanently. As soon as there was any hint of trouble, Peter dealt with it immediately in the most diplomatic way possible.

After sales passed the fifty-million-dollar mark Peter introduced an employee profit-sharing plan. Fifteen percent of the gross earnings of DIM Inc. was channeled into a bank account called the *EPS Fund*.

Once a month, the money from this account was divided up amongst all the personnel, calculating the average number of hours each employee worked to determine each one's share. This additional payment was a welcome monthly bonus to all the staff.

Peter explained the new payment procedure at one of their monthly company meetings. The *EPS Fund* payment was in lieu of salary increases. From now on wages would be permanently frozen. The *EPS Fund* would be their reward instead, Peter explained to his staff. It was intended as a collective incentive for all employees — instead of giving them individual merit increases.

All-in-all things at DIM Inc. could never be better.

CHAPTER 33

A radar alert prompted an emergency meeting at the Bayport office. "Take a look at this transfer sheet!" Henri handed Peter a document. "Notice the items I've highlighted in yellow."

Peter took the transfer sheet and gave it a cursory glance to familiarize himself with the layout. The report was a list of shareholders who had purchased shares in DIM Inc. during the past three months. Most of the listings were for modest purchases, a hundred shares or less, but the highlighted items were for large share purchases.

Henri leaned forward and explained, "This report shows that we now have *five* shareholders ... each one owning more than 4% of our company's total stock. You see ... look at this one. *DD Investments* now owns 4.3% of our total stock. Now look down here. *Hardy Planners* now owns 4.7% of our stock. And there are three more. Can you believe it, Peter? I'm not an expert in the stock market, but does this seem normal, to suddenly have five relatively new shareholders each owning this much stock?" Henri's voice was tense.

Peter glanced worriedly up and down the stock report reviewing the highlighted items. "Are any of these investors listed on our last quarterly report?"

"No. None of them! That's what got me worried. Why would five different people suddenly want to buy so much of our stock. Within three months each of them have a made a toehold purchase. Do you think I should look into it?"

"Absolutely!" Peter sensed this was trouble. "If these investors were not on our last annual report, this means they are all *new* investors. Once they own 5% of the total shares they will have to report to the Securities Exchange Commission. But even until that happens, we can't ignore this, Henri."

Peter looked up from the report and said, "Let's face it, our sales are rapidly increasing. Even though I've done my best to keep the business low-key, DIM is getting popular. I can see why investors might want to invest in the company. What I don't understand is why five different investors had the same idea ... at the same time!"

Peter tossed the report on top of the ebony coffee table. "Try to find out more about these investors, will you."

"First thing tomorrow morning, boss," Henri laughed.

"Maybe it's nothing to worry about," mumbled Peter to himself.

"You're probably right," appeased Henri, although his gut-instinct said differently.

*   *   *

Henri and Peter spent the remainder of the morning planning the marketing campaign for DIM 2.0 which was scheduled for release in six months. As the campaign planning progressed, they soon forgot about the stock report.

CHAPTER 34

"Wow! Look at that!" Julie exclaimed. "DIM 2.0 shows only 150 results. That's way better than the 108,000 results the search-engine brought up. DIM 2.0 eliminated more than 90% of the first set of results."

Alex and Julie were testing the new prototype of DIM 2.0 by trying out online searches and then converting them into DIM's format.

"This is marvelous, Julie. There is no search-engine on the Internet that can reduce the results to such a manageable number. This is going to make our new model a better way for doing online searches than using a search-engine by itself."

Alex said, "As Peter pointed out at our last session, this new DIM 2.0 model could revolutionize the way people search the Internet. Because you can save the results, you don't have to keep doing the same searches over and over again. Look ... I'll save these results in our Search Directory." Alex saved the file. "Now ... I'll open up the file ... and voilà... we have our results back again!"

They were testing the new prototype before they showed Peter what they had accomplished on the new version. *Won't he be impressed!* Alex thought.

The external appearance of DIM 2.0 was similar to DIM 1.0. The only difference was the removable basket was now a pocket with a plastic flap.

It was the functions of DIM 2.0 where the differences lay. For one thing, a network card and a web-browser had been added to the programming. The main menu had been revamped to include a file management system that was easier to manage files. The memory capacity had been increased to allow for 1,000 GB of stored data.

The design of DIM 2.0 was kept top-secret. Only Peter, Henri, George and the designers knew about the project. Peter intended to keep it this way, until the day it was released.

After they had finished testing the new prototype, Alex covered the computer over with a gray plastic dust cover and wheeled the portable cart into a corner in the factory's boardroom.

CHAPTER 35

Henri took an evening flight aboard an AirWings plane departing Bayport's Skybird Airport and flying east to Greenvale's Pineview Airport.

Henri accepted a glass of fruit punch and a club sandwich from the hostess. He hadn't eaten since breakfast and was glad for a bit of nourishment. Afterwards, he rested comfortably in his seat looking out the window at the scenery below.

He could see a small lake beginning to shimmer from the light of the setting sun. The lake was dotted with sailboats. A ferry was making its way across the lake to a destination on the other side.

It was now 7:05 p.m.. He would arrive in Greenvale at 7:50 p.m..

As the twin-engine plane got closer to the valley, mist swirled by the window. The terrain below was like an evergreen roller coaster. With a good pair of binoculars a passenger on the plane could spot caves in the hills that were homes for wildcats and black bears that inhabited these unpopulated regions.

Suddenly the flat plains of Hidden Valley appeared thousands of feet below. Henri could see Snake River etching its course through the heart of the valley. He felt his stomach go up as the plane began to descend.

The plane landed with a chirp of smoking wheels at Pineview Airport. A few other small planes were already parked in front of the tiny terminal building. When the engines of the plane shut down, the silence was stunning.

Henri was the last of the passengers to disembark the plane. He slung his overnight bag over his right shoulder, grabbed his portfolio case in his left hand, and headed for the terminal.

Henri spotted Peter immediately in the visitor's waiting area. The two men shook hands and went promptly to Peter's car in the parking lot.

"Did you have a nice flight?" Peter asked cordially.

"You bet. Man that view is gorgeous."

"You're right. It's only a ten-minute drive to my house. The others are already there," Peter said as he put Henri's bag into the trunk of his car. And off they went.

*   *   *

Peter, Henri, Alex, and Julie sat in deck chairs around the patio next to the swimming pool in Peter's backyard. It had been a hot day and the air was still warm and humid. They spent the evening swimming and now each had a refreshing drink in hand.

"Let's get down to business, shall we," said Peter as he leaned forward in his lounge chair and plopped his drink down on the umbrella-covered table. "I wanted to meet here ... instead of at the factory ... so there could be no chance of anyone overhearing our conversation."

Peter looked at each person in the group. They were all waiting in suspense for him to continue. "Something has come up that you need to know about," he said earnestly.

Alex gave a nervous laugh and said jokingly, "What? Someone has made a clone of DIM?"

Peter shook his head and laughed back, "No. It's *worse* than that. Henri has discovered something in the company's recent stock report that you should be made aware of. I think it would be better for *him* to explain."

Henri, who was sitting in the center of the group, pulled out some sheets of paper from his portfolio. In a grave voice he began to tell everyone about his discovery. "It is one of my duties to study the transfer sheets of the company's stock sales. Generally, I look for any unusual activities. On the last report I noticed there are five new investors who each purchased close to 5% of our total company shares.

As you may or may not know, when an investor owns 5% of a company's stock they are required to make a disclosure to the Securities Exchange Commission, the company (which is us), and to the stock exchange (which is TechExchange). The reason for this is that 5% of the stock of a company is considered a *significant* share ownership. It gives the investor greater voting privileges at shareholder meetings."

Alex, who was sitting directly across from Henri, asked, "Do any of these investors own 5% of our stock yet?"

Henri gave him a puzzled look. "That's the strange part. They own just below the 5% mark, which puts them in the clear with the SEC. Here, take a look at this list. I made a copy for each of you." Henri handed each of them a list of the investors.

Alex whistled as he read down the list.

DD Investments	*4.3%*
Hardy Planners	*4.7%*
Oro Syndicate	*4.8%*
Stock Consulting	*4.5%*
Research Marketers	*4.2%*
TOTAL SHARES	*22.5%*

Henri continued with his explanation of the situation. "Peter asked me to look into these investors to try and find out why this was happening. So I did." Henri paused as if he were reluctant to continue. "Yesterday I discovered that *all* of these shares were purchased by the *same* stock-broker: Crane Brokerage. It is a firm located in Oroton. Peter and I think these investors might actually be the same person. If we are right, this means that someone in Oroton now owns 22.5% of our company's stock."

"That's not good!" Julie exclaimed.

Alex asked Peter, "But isn't that illegal to do?"

Peter shrugged his shoulders. It was obvious the new change in circumstance was weighing heavily on his mind. "I'm not sure. My guess is it probably isn't illegal, but it certainly is unethical. It also appears to be a careful plot. Whoever this person is has given careful instructions not to go over the 5% limit. This implies they are deliberately avoiding giving a disclosure to the Securities Exchange Commission ... which would tell us who they are."

Henri added, "You see, when an investor makes a disclosure to the SEC they are required to give details about themselves. This information becomes public. Whoever is behind these share purchases of our stock obviously doesn't want his or her identity to be known."

Julie inquired anxiously, "Why would they want to hide from us?"

Peter said casually, "My guess is .... so they can accumulate as much stock as they can and then initiate a takeover bid of our company."

"A takeover? You can't be serious." Alex was shocked. He looked from Peter to Henri and then back to Peter again.

Peter had never felt tenser in his life. It was as if all his worst fears were coming true. But for the sake of those who worked for his company, he had to remain calm and in control. "Actually, Alex, I'm not all that surprised that this is happening. Takeovers of small hi-tech firms are quite common. I have developed a Shark Repellent plan to try and save DIM Inc. If someone *is* trying to take over the company, we need to set up some defense measures."

Alex was still reluctant to face the truth. "Do you honestly think that's what is happening? Aren't we jumping to conclusions here?"

Peter nodded gloomily. "Yes. It looks as though someone might be preparing a hostile takeover of DIM Inc. There is no other explanation for these particular stock purchases. Do you think it's just a coincidence, Alex?" His annoyance was starting to show through.

"I guess not. It does seem suspicious all five investors have the same broker. And all these companies are from *Oroton*." Alex shook his sheet in the air.

Peter replied, "Precisely! If we act fast, we might be able to save the company. But I must warn you, if this investor already owns more than 22% of our stock ... it may already be too late."

"So what ideas do you have for a plan?" Julie urged Peter.

Peter drew in a long breath. "I made a list of things I'd like for us to do. If you have any ideas of your own, please tell me. We will need to pool all our resources together ... to try and save DIM Inc. from a takeover." He handed each member of the group a copy of his plan.

"There are four parts to the Shark Repellent plan:

"One. We are going to introduce a flood of shares onto the stock-market. We will offer existing shareholders a lower price for these shares than the current stock price. By doing this, we will make it more expensive for a raider to buy out our company. They would have to buy *more shares* than they normally would ... and they may not want to do this.

"Two. I am going to change the by-laws of our company so that a shareholder would need to own 70% of the shares of our company before they can take control of DIM Inc. This is higher than the usual 51% that is normally needed to control a company. If I do this now, it will make it more expensive for a raider to acquire these extra shares in a takeover.

"Three. We have to cut back on expenses. We need to find ways to save as much money as we can to help fight this battle. We need to set up an emergency reserve fund in a separate bank account, at another bank. If a takeover does take place, this will serve as a cushion of money to fall back on.

"Four. We are going to put the release of DIM 2.0 on hold, until further notice. I realize this might jeopardize our plans for future sales, but we have no choice. Now is *not* a good time to introduce a new version of the product onto the market. If a takeover is imminent, then we need to focus on the problem at hand."

After each person in the group read over the Shark Repellent plan they began to discuss ways to implement it. Tasks were assigned and deadlines set. Peter wanted to do as much as he could to save his company from a possible buy-out.

Henri offered, "I'll go through the files and remove anything we don't want anyone to have or see. Then I'll store them away."

Alex and Julie offered to study the accounts together with the bookkeeper, to see what expenses could be reduced or temporarily suspended.

"We must keep this situation confidential," Peter urged the team. "If word leaks out that DIM Inc. is ripe for a takeover, it might cause chaos with our shareholders and panic our employees. We need to keep our heads on our shoulders and get through this calmly."

"They might guess anyway," countermanded Henri, "Especially when we release a bunch of new stock. But unless they know the actual reason we are doing this, it should remain a secret for awhile."

The tension in the air could be cut with a knife. Even though this new development was nobody's fault, it had suddenly become everyone's responsibility.

CHAPTER 36

By July the Shark Repellent plan was in full effect. The only employee of DIM Inc. informed of the plan was George Peppard. Peter took George into his confidence to explain the situation to him and, as can be expected, George became alarmed. *Who wouldn't be?*

It was a good thing Peter did tell George about the problem because George offered Peter a brilliant suggestion. "Let's find out who this raider is," said George emphatically. "We can plant a spy in their organization and find out as much as we can about them. Maybe even figure a way to prevent a takeover ... if this is where things are leading to."

"That's a great idea, George," responded Peter. "We already know the name of the brokerage firm who bought the shares on behalf of the five investors. And we know the broker's office is located in Oroton. What we *don't* know is who requested the purchase of the shares. How can we go about finding this out?"

George was always on the ball. "Easy. Try checking with the stock exchange that handled the transaction. Find out any details you can from them. And try calling the brokerage. Speak anonymously to a secretary or someone. Get them to reveal the identity of their client. You might need to lie to do this. If you can get a name, it would make it easier to do a background check."

"Good thinking, George. I'll try that."

Peter instinctively knew the fate of his company depended on how well he handled this dilemma. Any idea might prove beneficial. He decided to start with an investigation of the brokerage firm that handled the sale of the shares. Using the DIM computer in his office at the factory, Peter did a search on "Crane Brokerage". Several items of interest showed up. One item was an article and a photograph of Bill Crane at a fund-raiser. In the photo were three other businessmen from the Oroton district. One of these men was a person by the name of Richard Orem Drekkel, CEO of Drekkel Corporation.

Peter decided to do a sub-search on this Drekkel person. What he found out filled him with a sense of dread. Richard Drekkel was a financial analyst who ran a service in Oroton giving advice on stock transactions.

Is this a coincidence? Peter mildly wondered. He instinctively knew this was the person behind the share purchases of DIM Inc..

When Peter had a name, address, phone number, and basic facts about Richard Drekkel, he called Henri at the waterfront office. "You'll never guess who our mystery investor might be."

Henri became attentive. "Who?"

Peter lowered his voice. "Have you ever heard of a businessman named Richard Drekkel?"

"*Dick* Drekkel? Are you serious? Isn't he the guy who made a killing on pay-per-click advertising on the Internet?"

"I don't know anything about that," Peter answered honestly.

Henri filled him in. "A few years ago some people made millions of dollars doing this type of marketing. Unfortunately Internet pay-per-click advertising is no longer considered socially acceptable. I'll bet Drekkel now has a tarnished reputation from having being involved in it. My guess is he is probably looking for a way to get *legit* again."

Peter caught the drift of what Henri was saying. "Yes ... by buying out *our* company. That way he can sell a quality product and get back on the good side of the public again."

Henri replied, "Exactly. Well at least now we know who is likely behind the investor scheme ... and possibly why. What else did you find out?"

Peter checked over his notes as he spoke to Henri. "He runs a subsidiary company specializing in market surveys. You know the kind they do in shopping malls ... the ones that annoy shoppers so much." Peter snickered. "Also, Drekkel began his career by running a financial planning business in Oroton. That's how he got started. This service has been in operation for fifteen years. According to my research, he is some kind of stock whiz helping people get rich."

Henri was piecing the pieces together in his mind. "That explains the dirty trick he played on us. By planting five leeches on our company stock, he is sucking up enough shares to take control over our company; all without a word to you ... or the SEC. It makes me wonder what his next move is going to be."

"I can tell you *exactly* what his next move is going to be, Henri," Peter responded sardonically. "He's going to put in a tender bid. And I'll bet he does it soon." He paused to take a deep breath. "Anyway, we'll just have to wait and see, won't we?"

"You're right, Peter. That's about all we can do. Thanks for calling. Let me know if anything else happens."

CHAPTER 37

On the night of the intruders there was no moon. They chose it deliberately to enhance their invisibility. There were two intruders. One was named Roy. The other was named Ron. Easy names to remember, if they were ever caught. But not tonight. There was no way the owner of the factory was ever going to phone the cops. That would create a big scene, which would be reported in the local newspaper the next day, and nobody wanted *that* to happen, did they? So unless the intruders started a fire, it was highly unlikely anyone would dial 9-1-1 tonight.

Roy and Ron started their midnight caper at the rear entrance of the factory building. Hey, why not? Rolling up a two-hundred-pound metal door was the easiest way to slip inside. All they needed was a crowbar, some muscle for leverage, a metal bar to hold the door up, and they were through.

After Roy and Ron rolled through the opening onto the floor they instinctively paused and waited. Years of experience had taught them this was the single most dangerous moment to watch out for. There could be a guard with a shotgun. There could be a growling dog with three-inch-long teeth. There could be the sound of a high-pitched alarm.

Roy and Ron gradually relaxed when they realized that none of these things happened. They were safe, so far.

The two intruders wore black overalls covered with pockets closed over by Velcro. On their heads were black-knit ski caps. Streaks of black grease covered their face and ears. They looked like a pair of black ghosts with only the whites of their eyes glowing in the dark.

Roy and Ron used a crude map of the factory to find the administrative area. They headed straight for the files. Using a flashlight they began sifting through the papers looking for documents. Their instructions were clear: "Don't make a mess! Get the documents! Get out!"

Everything went according to plan. In fifteen minutes Roy and Ron had a selection of papers folded and stuffed in their pockets. Now the two of them looked like a pair of astronauts ready for outer space.

They were so busy they never noticed the shadow moving near the south wall of the admin area. It wasn't until Roy felt a sharp claw digging into the calf of his leg that he let a loud, "Yoww!" When he glanced down two amber eyes were glaring up at him. He kicked at the cat.

Roy said to Ron, "We're done. Let's get outta here!" They slammed the file drawers closed and bolted towards the delivery door. Roy rolled out first. Ron rolled out second.

* * *

The next day George peeked into Peter's office at nine. "Got a minute?"

Peter was preoccupied with the problems on his mind. *What now?* He nodded to George and offered him a seat across from his desk.

"What's up, George?" Peter was barely civil.

"Last night an intruder went through our files. Some of them are missing and a few were out of sequence. I noticed muddy footprints near the cabinets this morning. At first I thought it might be a local burglar. But now I'm not so sure. I wonder if this Drekkel guy might have sent someone over here ... you know ... to spy on *us*."

Peter felt instantly worried. "Did you write up an incident report about this, George? I'd really like to read it."

"Yes I did ... earlier this morning." George pointed to Peter's over-flowing In basket. "It's in there ... somewhere." George gave a quiet chuckle.

Peter decided to change the subject. "As you can tell I'm swamped with work. I guess I have a bit of catching up to do. Speaking of spying, who would you recommend we send to do a little spying of our own, on Drekkel Corporation in Oroton?"

"What about Alex Wiley? He's the brave daring type. I'll bet he could find something out about this rival company."

"I'll ask him. I know he and Julie have been busy on the new version of DIM but maybe he could spare a little time out since the release is on hold. After all ... this is kind of important." *To say the least!*

* * *

Alex agreed to be the company spy on one condition: "I want to do it my way."

"OK," agreed Peter, happy to have someone else dealing with this problem. "Just let me know if you need any help."

Two days later Alex packed a suitcase and caught a commuter flight to Bayport and from there transferred to another flight to Oroton. When Alex arrived at his destination, it was shortly after supper on Thursday evening.

Alex checked in at the Hilton Hotel in Oroton for a two-night stay. He had a quick shower and then headed down to the dining-room for a bite to eat. He ordered a whole-wheat roll, Caesar salad, lasagna, and a bottle of imported beer. While he ate, he read the *Oroton Herald.*

The next morning Alex telephone Drekkel Corporation from his hotel room. He made an appointment for a half-hour session later that afternoon with a client service officer named Lucy Winfield, who worked in the Market Research division.

Alex's plan was to do a bit of fictitious market research on behalf of DIM Inc. He honestly doubted Drekkel would discover he was there. After all, was it typical for a CEO of a billion-dollar corporation to look into the particulars of a new client? *Not likely!* And what chance was there that Lucy Winfield knew about Drekkel's takeover plans? *Slim to none*, Alex guessed.

Alex arrived for his appointment fifteen minutes early. He used this time to wonder around the plush front lobby of Drekkel Corporation. *Wow!* He couldn't help but admire the elegant surroundings of the office emporium. Everything smelled of money and success.

When Alex made his way up to the Market Research department he was greeted warmly. "Won't you come in, Mr. Wiley." Lucy Winfield invited her new client into the cubicle booth she occupied.

"Please call me Alex," he said in a friendly voice and shook her hand. Alex reminded himself to make this meeting seem genuine.

When they were both comfortably seated Alex explained to Lucy that he wanted to do some market research for the company he worked for. "I work for DIM Inc. Perhaps you've heard of us. Our company sells a research computer."

"Yes I *have* heard of you." Lucy eyes shone with admiration. She knew it was important to establish a common bond with a new client. "We are actually ordering some of those computers ourselves ... for our offices here in Oroton."

I'm not surprised, Alex thought.

Alex smiled innocently at Lucy. He realized she knew nothing of the possibility of a takeover of DIM Inc. by the company she worked for. He decided to keep it that way.

They spent the next hour filling out questionnaires and trying to determine what would be the best marketing plan for DIM Inc. Alex learned a few tips on how to market the DIM computers from Lucy. He found the session very informative. It was a win-win session for both of them.

At the end of the half-hour Alex showed his appreciation by making a payment of $250. "Thanks for your time, Lucy. You've been very helpful. I don't suppose you can spare a few minutes of your time and give me a tour of your office, could you? And then could you show me the best way out of this maze ... back to the front lobby?" Alex gave a little laugh.

"I would be happy to." Lucy took him by the elbow and escorted him to the central elevators. They both went inside and Lucy pushed the P button. "Let's start at the top, shall we?"

CHAPTER 38

Peter was dreading Alex's return from Oroton. Personally he didn't want to find out about his enemy. What he really wanted was for Drekkel and this problem to go away.

Alex knocked on his office divider shortly after ten o'clock.

"Come in, Alex," Peter barked.

Alex came into the office and sat down in the visitor's chair across from Peter's desk. For a full minute he remained silent with only a mere ghost of a smile on his lips.

"Well?" demanded Peter impatiently when he saw that Alex wasn't speaking up.

Alex wasn't sure of the best way to break the news to Peter so he decided not to beat around the bush. "Look Peter... I'm not going to lie to you about Drekkel. If he *does* decide to takeover DIM Inc. ... my guess is ... he will do it with pocket change. They have money coming out of their ears out there. I found out Drekkel, personally, is worth more than three billion dollars. I hate to say it, Peter, but it doesn't look good for us."

"Don't say that!" Peter slapped his hand down on his desk. At the moment he felt like strangling Alex. He was used to Alex's jesting but this was one of those days he wasn't in the mood for it. "Whose side are you on anyway, Alex?"

Alex laughed and put his hands up in a gesture of surrender. "Just giving you the facts. You wouldn't want me to sugar-coat things, would you?"

"We're in serious trouble here, Alex. If that goon buys out our company, we might *all* end up unemployed. And that includes you! I've already been down that path. So has Julie Sanders. I'm pretty sure none of us want to end up in that boat again." Peter picked up a piece of paper on his desk, crumpled it into a ball, and tossed it into a waste basket near the doorway.

Alex was no business fool. He had watched his mother and father struggle to build their family business. He knew it wasn't all roses. But lying at a time like this could be risky. "My advice Peter is ... if you *do* sell the company ... get as much for it as you can!"

"Well thanks," Peter said sarcastically. "I'll keep that in mind!" He paused and took a deep breath. "Now tell me everything you found out ... and I mean everything!"

* * *

A short article appeared in *Today's News* relating to an increase in number of released shares for DIM Inc. A history of the company's stock prices was included. No speculation was offered as to the reason why these shares were being introduced. The article seemed almost inconsequential. It was one paragraph long.

CHAPTER 39

On the first day of September DIM Inc. became the target of a takeover by Drekkel Corporation. The official bid was announced to the management in the form of a tender offer. No one was surprised; their worst fears had been confirmed.

DIM Inc. had now been in business for almost four years. It employed two hundred and fifty-five employees. It cleared an annual profit of one hundred and ten million dollars. It was a rapidly-growing enterprise.

Peter decided it would be prudent to hold an emergency stockholders meeting at the factory. He set the time of the meeting for Friday night at 6:00 p.m. All the stockholders were invited to attend. This included Dick Drekkel who was now the lead shareholder. At the shareholders meeting Drekkel would be given an opportunity to present his tender offer, or "Saturday Night Special", as Henri called it.

Shareholders crowded in the factory to attend the meeting. Most of the employees of DIM Inc. were also present. All the available space in the building was cleared to accommodate the huge crowd.

Peter and Henri leaned against the railing of the loft surveying the madhouse below. People were shouting and shoving their way through the droves. The air was filled with tension and anticipation. *Was this meeting good news or was it bad news?*

At 6:10 p.m. Dick Drekkel climbed onto a wooden platform in the link area between the administrative area and assembly area. He took the microphone in his left hand.

"May I have your attention ... please!" Drekkel spoke in a loud clear voice.

Gradually the noise of the crowd began to quiet down.

"My name is Richard Drekkel. I own 22.5% of the stock of DIM Inc. I also own 75% of the stock of my own company, Drekkel Corporation, which is located in Oroton.

"I have asked the owner of DIM Inc., Peter Preston, for a chance to speak with you and to present you with an offer. I will be straight-forward and honest with you. I want you to consider selling your shares in DIM Inc. to me. I am offering a premium rate of $30.30 per share. This is $2 higher than the current market value of this stock. You also have the option to exchange your shares in DIM Inc. for an equivalent amount of shares in Drekkel Corporation, if you so choose."

Drekkel raised his hands to control the murmuring traveling throughout the crowd. "I'm going to be upfront about my offer. I want to buy your shares because I intend to take control over this company."

The crowd began talking loudly.

Drekkel waited for silence to resume. "I believe I can give DIM Inc. the best future possible. I plan to improve its value by making a long-term investment in this company. To show you that I am a fair businessman, I will outline the details of my offer."

The stockholders pressed closer and listened intently to what Drekkel had to say. They were well aware this meeting could affect their investments, and to some, their futures.

A flash from a camera went off as a journalist took a picture of Drekkel. Several other journalists were busy writing notes and one recorded the speech on a portable recording device.

Drekkel continued with his proposal. "Once I own this company, it is my intention to re-locate the factory to a brand-new facility in Oroton. There ... it will have state-of-the-art equipment. This will put it in a position to produce a higher volume of computers ... maybe even ten times more than the company presently produces.

"According to my sources, 32% of the investors of DIM Inc. are actually employees of the company. I will invite each of these employee-investors to relocate to the new company site in Oroton ... when the time comes.

"In addition, all present managers of this company will be encouraged to apply for new positions ... although I cannot guarantee that any, or all of them, will be hired.

"Twenty percent of the shares of DIM Inc. are presently owned by the current CEO, Peter Preston. In the terms of this offer today, I am prepared to pay him the generous sum of $140 million dollars for his portion of the shares.

"Now, it is your choice to accept or refuse my offer. I strongly urge you accept it. It could mean a great future you and for this innovative company. It would also mean you would make a bundle of money ... when you sell your shares to me."

At this point Drekkel let out a laugh as though he were trying to lighten the tension in the crowd. A scattering of shareholders began to applaud the speaker.

Drekkel asked if they had any questions.

"What is the deadline for your offer, Mr. Drekkel?" asked a stockholder from Bayport.

"October 31st. That's about a couple of months away." Drekkel sensed the mood of the crowd starting to swing in his direction. It gave him added confidence.

"If your offer is rejected, do you plan to make a new offer?" someone from the front row asked.

Drekkel laughed and shook his head. "Now that would be telling, wouldn't it? You'll just have to wait and see." He secretly hoped to achieve his goals with this initial bid but kept that plan to himself.

"Do you plan to keep the product name, if you become the owner of the company?" asked an elderly employee of DIM Inc..

"For the time being, yes I do. The product is already popular. The name is recognizable. Why mess with a good thing?" What Drekkel didn't say to the shareholders was that he *did* intend to create a new name for the product. He also planned to alter the product design slightly. But why confuse everyone at this stage of the game?

Not even the slickest politician with the most alluring campaign could surpass the level of charisma exuded by Dick Drekkel at this emergency stockholders meeting. By the time the meeting was over, he had convinced many of them of the worth of his plan.

* * *

It was nine o'clock when the meeting was finally over and all the shareholders had left. Peter and Henri were drinking brandy in the loft and discussing the effects the takeover bid might have on them. Peter was actually relieved that everything was out in the open. His suspicions were at last confirmed and the situation could be dealt with.

"What did you think of the offer, Henri?" Peter asked sincerely.

"Well ... I can say this ... it was no *stink bid*. It was a fair and generous offer. I was surprised the raider came to the meeting himself ... instead of sending a rep in his place. But did you think he was being completely honest? I got the feeling he was missing out some crucial details." Henri had been sweating a little over the problem too and found some stress-relief by drinking a glass of brandy Peter kept stocked in the loft.

"Do you think they'll accept it?" Peter prodded his friend and business associate for some insight.

"You bet I do. Who wouldn't? Especially since he is allowing the employee-investors to get new jobs at a brand-new facility. Often employees lose their jobs during the restructuring stage following a takeover. Now nobody can complain that he is making them unemployed. It is a clever tactic on his part."

Peter didn't want to rush into a decision himself. "I'm going to have to think about the offer myself. Until today, I had no intention of selling the company. I mean I started this business right from a concept, Henri. Yesterday, if he had asked me, I would refuse to sell my stake in the company. But with Drekkel owning 22%, I have no choice but to at least consider it. He does have an edge over us, doesn't he?"

"You bet he does! And it is a good thing you realize it. If he only owned 5%, or even 10% of the stock, we might be able to fight

THE SECRET COMPANY IN HIDDEN VALLEY

him off. But 22% ... that's a different story. That's almost a quarter of the control."

Peter found himself again facing another unexpected change in his life. When he had lost his job at Dale University, he had proceeded willingly into a new venture. And he had succeeded at it. Now, once again, he was being forced to face an unknown future. It did not sit well with him. He was too conservative in his ways to handle the uncertainty this situation presented.

There was a real possibility he would lose his company. This made him feel numb inside. Was it shock? Was it worry?

Peter blamed himself for letting this happen although he knew it really was Drekkel's fault. "If only I could have seen it coming ... before it got this far," he berated himself.

Henri took a sip from his snifter. "It's not your fault, Peter," as though reading his friend's mind. "Whatever happens, I want you to know that I'm on *your side*. Even if that snake-in-the-grass offered me a million dollars, I wouldn't work for his company out there in the desert."

Peter wondered if it was just the booze talking or was Henri really this dedicated. All the same, it was nice to hear. Besides he owed Henri for starting the company. If it hadn't been for that first television infomercial DIM might never have gotten off the ground.

"Thanks, Henri," Peter said soberly. "That means a lot to me."

CHAPTER 40

Within the following two weeks Drekkel was able to purchase 17% more shares from the stockholders. This made him the owner of 39% of DIM Inc.'s total stock.

The more shares he acquired, the more eager Drekkel became at the prospect of owning the company. He reminded himself of the fact that this new hi-tech company sold one of the most talked-about products. Every day there were new ways discovered to use the research computer. One loyal fan of DIM had put up a website devoted entirely for sharing ideas on how to use the DIM computer. This website recorded more than one million hits at day.

Because of the low profile Peter Preston had taken, and because of the prehistoric conditions of the assembly factory, Drekkel had developed a condescending attitude towards the present owner of DIM Inc. He perceived Peter as a naive computer geek without much business savvy. What Drekkel didn't know was that Peter Preston had once been a computer-science professor.

As the deadline for the initial offer came close to expiring, Drekkel began to pressure Peter to sell his bulk of the shares. Every day something appeared in Peter's office trying to coax him to sell his 20% of the shares. Phone calls. Letters. E-mail messages. *It's for the best. Hey, one hundred and forty million dollars is nothing to sneeze at. Give up, Preston! You know you're going to lose in the end.* Things like that.

* * *

Drekkel's goal became closer to fulfillment. On October 31st he owned 63% of the total number of the company shares. Another 7% and he would have controlling interest.

The revised company's by-laws forced him to need 70% of the total shares before he could exercise control over the business. This turned out to be a positive feature of the Shark Repellent plan.

* * *

On November 5th Drekkel made a second tender offer to the shareholders of DIM Inc. It was similar to the first one except the premium price was upped to $40.40 per share. The buy-out offer for Peter's 20% increased to $170 million dollars. A new deadline was set for November 30th.

The lure to sell their shares grew stronger as the remaining shareholders realized Drekkel was now very close to controlling the company. One way or the other he was going to be their new boss.

By the end of the month the only shares left to sell were Peter's private stock of 20%. He had coolly refused the second offer. *Fuck you, Drekkel!*

Drekkel became belligerent. Three and four times a day he left messages on Peter's answering machine. The messages were more like threats really. Owning 80% of the shares gave Drekkel a new sense of power.

The pressure to sell began to cave in around Peter like the buckling hull of a sunken ship beneath the sea. There was no time left to rescue his beloved company. He felt like he was sinking too.

Even his own mind began to betray him with luring promises. He wouldn't need to work anymore. He could travel and see the world. He would be able to comfortably retire. *Wasn't that the dream of most people; to quit while they were ahead?* The money from the sale of his shares would keep him comfortable for the rest of his life. He could sit by his swimming pool all day and write his memoirs. After running a successful business, that would be stimulating. *Wouldn't it?*

Peter could almost feel DIM crying out to him. He had designed DIM. He had brought DIM to life. He had made DIM a success. DIM was his and should not belong to anyone else.

Peter could feel his control over the company dissolving like an iceberg in a summer Arctic sea. He was losing the battle fast. And he was powerless to stop it.

I'm sorry DIM. I didn't see this coming.

Peter sensed Drekkel waiting in every corner of his life. He could feel an invisible pair of eyes studying his every move. With each passing day Peter's resolve began to weaken.

If I lose DIM I'm out!

Peter panicked at the thought of losing the company he had developed over the years. Running the business was what he did now. He couldn't imagine doing anything else. It absorbed all of his time. It was the main focus of his life. Going from company president to retiree was too drastic a change.

He refused all of Drekkel's calls.

One morning, before the holiday season began, Veronica Hill contacted Peter by phone and sweetly informed him Richard Drekkel wanted to speak to him. She said it was urgent and Peter reluctantly accepted the call.

"What do you want, Drekkel?"

"You know what I want, Preston. I now own 80% of the stock of your company. Or should I say *my* company. What's it going to take to get you to sell me your shares?" Drekkel breathed heavily like an obscene phone-caller.

"My first response is to say to you ... over my dead body ... but since that would be right up your alley, Drekkel, my answer is this: *Two ... hundred ... million ... dollars.*"

Peter could hear a gasp of annoyance on the other end of the line. He held the phone away from his ear expecting a blast of foul language. To his surprise there was only dead silence. Until he heard one quiet word. "OK," Dick said nonchalantly. "If that's what it will take ... that's what I'll give you. Let my secretary know what bank you deal with out there in Greenvale. I'll arrange for the funds to be transferred into your account. It was good doing business with you, Preston."

There was click and a pause and then Veronica came back on the line. She obtained the necessary banking details from Peter and hung up.

And that was that! This completed the sale of DIM Inc. to Drekkel Corporation. Peter thought it was ironic how something that took four years to create was gone in less than four minutes.

CHAPTER 41

True to his word, Drekkel transferred two hundred million dollars into Peter's bank account at the *Premium Banking Center* in Greenvale. But Peter felt no satisfaction in receiving the payment. To him it was "blood money" and the blood was from the murder of DIM Inc..

The moving date was set for December 31st. The end of the year. The end of his business.

For Peter it was too soon. He wasn't ready to make the adjustment yet. He needed more time. He needed to find a way to reverse the takeover and be in charge again. *Where is my White Knight?*

He felt completely reluctant to start the packing process. Wandering aimlessly throughout the factory building, gazing at all the equipment that would have to go, Peter didn't even know where to begin. Once again he knew this was one of those times when he lacked motivation because he had been forced into something he didn't want to do.

If DIM was a pet, what would he say? *Sorry, old boy, it's time for you to get a new owner?* He had made a mistake somewhere and this was all happening because of that mistake. But where had he done wrong?

If only his foggy brain could become clear again, maybe he could find a way out of this mess. And DIM could stay. And he could be the boss again. *Dream on.*

When the end of the month came the assembly plant was boxed up and made ready to be shipped out to its new facility in Oroton. Peter supervised the move by barking out orders. "Hey, be careful with that!" "Don't put that there!" He was in a rotten mood.

Two of the moving men pushed passed Peter knocking him to the side. They were wheeling a laden dolly towards the shipping and receiving ramp and pretended not to see him. Normally a jolt like that wouldn't have bothered Peter, but this morning it set him off. "Hey! Watch what your doing!" Peter shouted at the workmen. *Ignorant bozos!*

The boxes were put on the conveyor belt and wheeled from there to the dark confines of one of the moving trucks. The truck looked like a giant shark swallowing DIM up whole.

It took nearly six hours to disassemble the plant and load everything into the trucks. They would be bound for the city of Oroton five hundred miles west of Greenvale. Peter thought they might as well be taking his company to the moon.

In his sensible mind Peter knew this was just business. *What am I getting so upset over? I shouldn't be reacting to the takeover so personally.* Right from the start he had been aware the business world could be unpredictable. He had been determined not to be a naive entrepreneur. And now here he was losing his cool.

During the negotiations Drekkel had slyly reasoned with Peter: "DIM deserves a more sophisticated factory." Peter had agreed. The old factory building was never intended to be permanent home anyway. *But why did Drekkel have to be the one to give DIM a better home?*

After everything was loaded the trucks ambled across the parking lot swaying from side to side with their ill-gotten burden. They disappeared down the narrow driveway and out of sight. The taillights of the last truck winked on and off through the trees.

"Good-bye, DIM," Peter whispered as he watched helplessly from the front door of the factory.

CHAPTER 42

The pain of the loss of DIM Inc. sank like a knife into Peter's heart. There were no words to describe the hurt he felt inside. He was in a state of anguish. He felt devastated. Only a grieving parent who had lost a child to a kidnapper could understand what Peter was going through.

Over and over he thought of DIM. He remembered creating DIM and investing his life-savings into the start-up costs for DIM Inc. He remembered devoting his days and nights to the operation of the business. Like a faithful father Peter had watched over his enterprise, took it through its trials and tribulations, and made it a success.

Did he really think he could take the two hundred million dollars and say "business is business"? Or was the money supposed to be putty to fill the empty gap rapidly growing inside him?

Each time Peter thought about DIM Inc. a feeling of grief overwhelmed him. He was helpless against the loss. It welled up inside him like a tidal wave.

His company was gone. It would never be coming back. DIM Inc. no longer existed. He might as well put a headstone on the property that said R.I.P..

Knowing that Drekkel was a devious businessman who had stolen the company out from under him didn't help. DIM had been his responsibility and he had failed in protecting it. That was the real truth. His conscience would not allow him to escape this fact.

Nobody could reverse the takeover and that's what Peter really wanted to happen. He wanted a white knight to come to DIM's rescue. No white knight came though.

Everything in the old building was cleared out except for the office equipment in the administrative area. Each day Peter dutifully left home in the morning and drove to work. He couldn't seem to let go of this routine. But as the business wound down he found he had less and less to do. Most days he just sat at his desk staring off into outer space and rubbing a three-day growth of beard.

The two hundred million dollars sat idle in the bank in Greenvale collecting a hefty daily interest. Peter wanted nothing to do with the money. He had become resentful of it. It was as if a bad magic spell had been cast over the money. Peter was sure spending it would bring further doom into his life. So he just left it there.

Peter's footsteps echoed inside the vacant building as he walked across the floor. From the window in the employee's lunchroom Peter could see the empty bird feeders swinging in the breeze. Even the birds had left. He had never felt more alone in his life.

CHAPTER 43

Henri Larue had two months left on his original contract so he decided to stay on at the waterfront office and wrap things up there. The direct-factory sales system was being phased out. He would have to find another contract somewhere else.

There was one bit of good news in the midst of the fiasco. Alex and Julie surprised everyone by announcing their engagement to be married. The wedding was set for July 15th. Invitations were sent to family and friends.

Melanie Gold was busy running her successful desktop-publishing business, Gold Advertising. She had hired an assistant. She was shocked when she read about the takeover of DIM Inc. in the newspaper. Melanie tried calling Peter to offer her condolences but was unable to reach him. Maybe she would get a chance to talk to him at the wedding.

James Wiley heard about the takeover from a business colleague while they were having lunch at his country club. "That's too bad," James said insincerely to his friend. He couldn't even pretend to feel sorry it had happened. James decided not to mention to his colleague that his son Alex was a former employee of this unfortunate firm since it didn't rank as a need-to-know piece of information. *Why spoil my reputation? They probably got what they deserved!*

* * *

DIM went to Oroton along with fifty of the former employees, including George Peppard. George had been hired as Director of Operations of the new subsidiary company, DIMKEL. That was the new company name.

The assembly plant for the DIMKEL computers was located in a state-of-the-art building in the industrial division of Oroton. The size of the building was one hundred thousand square feet. Everything in it was brand-spanking new. All the equipment was carefully laid out to begin the manufacturing of the computers.

DIMKEL was the first manufacturing business Drekkel had owned. He quickly learned what a challenge it was to operate one. The magnitude and complexity of the facility required a team of professionals to get it up-and-running.

Drekkel had no intention of doing direct-factory sales. In his opinion it was an inferior method of processing orders. It conjured up images of a hokey home business. Drekkel wanted his new company to be truly sophisticated. To hell with the efficiency of direct-factory sales; his heart was set on retail.

Three million dollars was invested in the marketing campaign to promote the revamped DIMKEL computers. There were magazine ads, billboards, and complimentary coupons. A lot of effort went into arranging sales through retail store-chains. By the time production began, DIMKEL had pre-orders for more than one million units. Drekkel was pleased with this early progress.

*   *   *

Veronica Hill was not at all pleased with the takeover. After years of idolizing her boss, she now saw a different side of him. And it wasn't a side she liked. When she found out how he had tricked the shareholders of DIM Inc. by setting up separate brokerage accounts, and secretly buying up shares, her respect for Mr. Drekkel took a major downslide.

How could he do such a thing?

Veronica continued working as an executive assistant for Drekkel Corporation but much of her enthusiasm had diminished. It wasn't that she was against a person making money or anything; she just didn't like seeing someone cheat to do it.

Every morning she went to work but instead of making her boss a cup of coffee she only made herself one instead. She no longer popped into his office to chat with him or give him a cheery hello. The thought of rubbing his shoulders now gave her the creeps.

Her unhappiness grew daily. Veronica realized the takeover made DIM Inc. now belong to Drekkel Corporation. This bad mistake was not ever going to get undone. Veronica's sense of common decency had been offended by the takeover. It left a disappointed feeling inside of her that wouldn't go away.

Maybe I should get another job, she decided one day. She needed to believe in the company she worked for. It was hard to put in an honest day of work when you knew they were a bunch of buccaneers.

"I'll give it another month," Veronica promised herself. After that, if she still felt the way she did now, she would spruce up her résumé and make an exit.

*   *   *

George Peppard stood in the center of the new manufacturing facility in Oroton. The first orders were beginning to roll out. It felt good watching production begin again.

George had rationalized his decision to accept the job offer as Director of Operations much in the same way Peter Preston had convinced himself to sell his shares to Dick Drekkel. Sure it sounded like a good deal, and seemed to be a sensible financial decision, but deep in this gut George knew it was the worst mistake he had ever made.

It was too late to change his mind now. His family had recently bought a home in Oroton. He could hardly go to his wife now and say it didn't feel right working under the new management. *A job's a job,* she was likely to say. And that would end that conversation.

George did admit his new annual salary of 275K was part of the lure to accept the offer. It meant living a better lifestyle. It meant taking vacations to exotic places. It meant sending his two children to private schools. *Who could complain about that?*

Still, George missed the old factory. It had been a mysterious almost magical place to work in. There was always something thrilling happening there. Unlike the sterility of the Oroton facility, the old factory had been alive and virile.

The new facility was a slick fully-automated industrial complex with absolutely no personality. There was no room in it for any imagination. It had been designed to produce a maximum amount of orders, with a minimal expenditure — and that was all. It was not intended to be a source of fulfillment or inspiration.

When George attended the first company meeting he quickly caught on: *he was there to listen only*. Nobody asked for his opinion. Even though he was supposed to be the director of operations, he was only given orders. The message was loud and clear, "Do as you're told, or you're out!"

George sent Peter a postcard of the new facility. He had a stack of them in his office. On the back of a postcard George wrote: "This is the Oroton assembly facility. The new company name is DIMKEL. Trust you are well. George."

CHAPTER 44

Wiley Estate Gazebo, July 15th, 4 p.m.

The wedding was held in the gazebo on the Wiley estate. The ceremony was performed at four o'clock on Saturday afternoon in the presence of one hundred invited guests. The weather was hot and sunny with no rain in the forecast.

Julie wore a mid-calf white dress that had been hand-made for the occasion. In her braided hair was a garland of white orchids. She wore a pair of delicate white sandals over her bare feet. In keeping with a look of simplicity, she held a cluster of orchids in her ungloved hand.

Alex's tuxedo was black with white satin lapels. A recent trip to the barber had his hair perfectly groomed. His black patent-leather shoes gleamed like mirrors. In the buttonhole of his lapel was a single orchid, taken from Julie's bouquet.

Julie's sister Jasmine was the maid-of-honor. Peter Preston was the best man. Julie's father was the bride's escort. Annette, Alex's niece, was the flower-girl.

The gazebo could only hold ten people. The remaining guests stood around the circumference of the gazebo. The pentagon-shaped building was freshly painted and had flowers hanging in the openings. A bright blue runner carpet was laid down the center of the gazebo and steps, for the bridal party to walk on.

The wedding couple spoke their own written vows. The words described how the couple had met, how their relationship had evolved, and why they decided to marry. It was a story both of them wanted to keep as a legacy with their wedding memorabilia.

Julie designed the matching set of wedding rings. Each ring was sterling silver with a blue diamond embedded in the center. The larger one was for Alex; the smaller one for Julie. Alex teased her saying they were "magic rings" and now he would always know where she was — through the rings, of course.

After the couple spoke their vows, and sealed their future together with a soft intimate kiss, Julie threw her bouquet of orchids into the crowd behind them. Katherine Wiley caught the bouquet.

A fountain of champagne was set up next to the swimming pool. H'or d'oeuvres were served by the Wiley household staff dressed in prim black-and-white uniforms. The guests mingled by the pool.

James Wiley, the proud father of the groom, gave a toast to the couple and presented Alex with a cheque for fifty thousand dollars. "For your future together, son," James said in an eloquent voice.

Irene Wiley was pleased with her son's choice of a mate. She saw the wedding as a sign that if you believed in others all would turn out well. Her patience with Alex was proof of this point. She wished them a wonderful life together.

At seven o'clock in the evening a dance began on the terrace. All the doors of the mansion were propped wide open to allow the guests to come and go, dance, mingle and socialize.

The hot day turned into a lovely warm evening. The moon was full adding to the romantic atmosphere of the special occasion. Fortunately, there were only a few mosquitoes out, so the guests were able to lounge by the pool well into the night.

At the stroke of midnight, the wedding couple jumped into Alex's BMW that had a "Just Married" sign mounted on the back with paper flowers pinned to the sides of the car. After waving goodbye to the guests, the couple drove up into the hills to the Secret Hideaway resort where they planned a weeklong honeymoon.

CHAPTER 45

Peter sat alone in the boardroom of the factory wondering what to do. Out of the corner of his eye he noticed a cart with a dust cover over it sitting in the corner. The cart was partially hidden by one of the palm plants. He got up from his chair and went over to it. *What is this?*

He wheeled the cart into the middle of the room and removed the dust cover. It was a computer. Peter instantly realized it was the prototype for DIM 2.0. This was the model Alex and Julie had been working on prior to the takeover.

I wonder if it works.

Peter plugged the unit in and turned on the power switch. He connected the modem of the computer to his satellite converter to allow access to the Internet. A few seconds later the computer booted-up and the opening screen came to view. He pulled up a chair and sat facing the unit.

Following the easy instructions in the opening screen, Peter tried out a simple online search. He watched the results appear from the search-engine. Then he did a second DIM search to fine-tune the results. He watched the results appear.

Amazing!

He set up a directory for the results. It wasn't long before he figured out all the ins and outs of using DIM 2.0. Peter could feel the potency of the new model as he performed search after search. No wonder Alex and Julies were so keen with they were developing it.

DIM 2.0 proved to be a better method of doing online searches than using the combination of an ordinary PC, web-browser, and search-engine. It wasn't long before Peter saw what Alex had seen; DIM 2.0 was not just beneficial as a research computer; it was an *alternative* to an ordinary PC. Since most people used their PC's mainly for surfing the Internet, they could easily get by with only a DIM 2.0 computer.

It was one thing to make a better product than the original DIM computer. It was another thing to make a product that was better than a PC itself. Peter felt proud of this.

The contract for the sale of DIM Inc. to Drekkel Corporation had not included any stipulations over other versions of DIM. In fact, Dick Drekkel didn't know DIM 2.0 even existed. This awareness gave Peter a secret pleasure.

You might have stolen the mother, Drekkel, but you didn't get the baby!

*   *   *

Later that afternoon Peter fell asleep on one of the comfortable lawn chairs underneath the patio umbrella. He wore a blue and white bathing suit and used a rolled-up towel for a pillow. It was stifling hot. The temperature was almost a hundred degrees in the shade. There had been no rain in the valley for twenty straight days.

While Peter slept he had a vivid dream.

He and Henri were in the waterfront office in Bayport. They were both sitting in chairs facing a huge window with their feet propped up on the ledge. They were smoking cigars, drinking beer, and laughing. Henri kept calling Peter a "wizard" and saying what a genius he was. Peter was feeling extremely pleased with himself.

Then the dream suddenly changed.

Everything went dark and cold. Suddenly Peter was lying alone on the floor of the factory staring up at the ceiling. He felt chilled all over. He could see bats flying overhead. He felt powerless to get up. It was as if he a ten-ton weight sitting on top of him. To his right he could see a bright light. He knew it was a doorway to the outside world. The light was attractive and Peter wanted to get up and go towards the light. But something prevented him and kept him trapped on the floor.

Peter suddenly woke up drenched in sweat.

"What a dream!" he said out loud. He tried to shake the images out of his head but they wouldn't leave. Peter dragged himself out of the lawn chair and dove into the cool water of the swimming pool. The shock of the water felt good. Soon he was wide awake again.

After swimming lazily for ten minutes, Peter climbed aboard a floating pool chair and lay there looking up into the cloudless blue sky.

What did that dream mean?

First he was laughing and celebrating and then suddenly he was all alone in the dark.

And why was Henri calling me a wizard?

Peter knew he was no wizard. He was intelligent but not especially gifted. But wait a minute! *He* might not be a wizard, but DIM certainly was. DIM was the amazing genius.

Peter smiled to himself, "Maybe I should have called DIM ... *The Wizard.*"

Peter sat up abruptly in the pool chair. In an instant it dawned on him what the dream was telling him. The name of the new version DIM 2.0 should be *The Wizard.*

Peter's mind began to spiral. Things were flying together. A plan was beginning to form. He could set up a new company. He could use the new version of DIM as the product. He could modify the new version to make it look different from the original.

Nobody would have to know there was any link between The Wizard and the original version of DIM. Let people think it was a clone. There was nothing illegal about creating a clone; plenty of companies did it.

Peter's imagination went into full swing. He imagined withdrawing some of the two hundred million dollars from his bank account and using the money to start the new business. He imagined selling The Wizard computers and it becoming an overnight sensation. And do you know why? The Wizard would be a better product than DIM because of its online search capabilities.

The Wizard would become a competitor its own former product. The idea suddenly seemed fantastic to him … and funny too!

Peter knew there was nothing wrong with someone starting a competitor company. The only thing unusual about this situation was that competitor companies didn't usually belong to the original owner. But hey, nobody needed to know that, did they?

I'll keep that tiny fact to myself.

There was no condition in the takeover contract stating that Peter couldn't start another business selling a similar product. Peter was sure any person could create a clone of DIM and sell the product as a new business. It may be slightly unethical to do this, but it wasn't actually illegal.

So why not him?

He would become a competitor of his own former company. He would sell the new product and make a fortune doing it. One top of this, he would use the two hundred million dollars Drekkel had given him to launch this new company.

Now that was poetic justice!

"Yes!" Peter shouted up to the sky.

He felt instantly liberated. He got out of the pool and quickly dried himself off with his towel. Then he trotted into the house and headed straight for the study.

Peter grabbed up a pad of paper and a pen from his desk and flopped down on the leather couch ignoring the fact that he was still wet. Before the ideas could vanish from his mind, he quickly wrote them down.

Plan B...

CHAPTER 46

"What do wizards signify?" Peter asked himself.

One word came immediately to mind: *Magic!* Wizards were synonymous with magical occurrences. For hundreds of years wizards were the focus of folklore, fables, and legends relating to magic. Wizards were often symbolized as wise men who could advise the best paths in life to take. They were envisioned as higher beings. People in ancient times consulted wizards for advice on many different subject matters. Wizards were considered "sages" with advanced intellectual capabilities. They were akin to modern-day super-heroes except wizards had skills in areas of wisdom and magic rather than in feats of physical strength.

Everyone loved magic, especially children. It was the treasured belief in magic that kept the world running. Peter knew if he used a magic theme in the development of The Wizard it might make the computers popular with youths. So he planned the following:

Idea 1 - The screen-saver would be an animated little wizard in the center of the screen, holding a magic wand, ready to perform any request on behalf of its operator.

Idea 2 - Each screen would open with a *kaleidoscope* rainbow of colors beginning at the center of the screen and spreading out to the corners before showing the actual screen results.

Idea 3 - The cursor would be a little wand instead of the usual arrow that most PCs had. This would make the operator "the magician" who made things happen.

Idea 4 - The unit color would be royal blue and have flecks of gold in the enamel paint.

Idea 5 - The name of the computer would be *The Wizard*.

Idea 6 - The name of the company would be *Wizard Computers*.

Idea 7 - There would be a 24-hour hotline of Tech Support at: *1-888-*Wizard*.

All of the features of the original DIM computer would be included in The Wizard in addition to the new online search capabilities. The layout of the screens would be different to mask the fact that there was any relation between the two computer models.

An extensive database library would be accessible via a secure Internet website for customers only. This would allow the operator to download databases they wished to have by using a password. This was a step up from DIM's catalogue system.

*　　*　　*

Night and day Peter worked on the new project. It was thrilling to be back in action again. All his feelings of depression evaporated. Peter Preston was back in the driver's seat.

Like many people, Peter found it difficult to admit when he was wrong. But now, with his future glowing with promise and hope, it was easier for him to admit his former mistakes. He realized the moment he had lost control over DIM Inc. was when he had decided to go public with the company. He should never have put the company shares on the stock market. That was how the cunning Drekkel had found a way to buy his company. If Peter had kept the company private he would probably still be the owner of DIM Inc. today. It was a hard lesson to learn.

Peter decided Wizard Computers would be a 100% privately-owned company. He wanted to share the company with the people who had helped make DIM happen; Alex, Julie, and Henri. He decided to offer each of them a part-ownership in Wizard Computers. With four responsible owners, who had experience running a technology business, the new company was bound to thrive.

The first person Peter approached with the partnership idea was Henri Larue. Henri was stunned by Peter's plan. "You want to set up a competitor company? Are you serious? Drekkel will kill you!"

"Not right away, he won't." Peter laughed. "He won't even know it's me. If we kept the location of the factory a secret for two years, we can keep this new company under wraps too." Peter was feeling smug and pleased with his new plan. "So ... do you want in or not?"

Henri agreed but on one condition. "I want it to be an *equal* partnership, amongst the four of us" he insisted as he spoke to Peter in the reception area of the waterfront office. "This isn't just about money. When you put your ideas into a company, and that company becomes a success *because* of those ideas, and makes millions of dollars, you know you should be rewarded with more than with just a salary or a commission. Take DIM Inc., for example. *You* invested the money to start the business, but it was *my* idea to do the infomercial that launched the business. So, if you want me in as a partner, it has to be with the four of us as *equal* partners. Each owns 25% of the new company. We keep it private. We don't bother incorporating it since we won't be going public anyway. What do you say?"

Peter instantly liked the idea. With four equal partners the responsibilities would also be divided equally. He would never have the worries entirely on his own shoulders again. "I tell you what, Henri. Let's get the four of us together and we'll vote on it. If the vote is a unanimous "Yes" then that's what we will do. But if even one person votes *No* we forget the whole thing."

It was these little challenges that got Henri involved in the company in the first place. "You're on!"

*   *   *

Alex and Julie loved the idea of a partnership, as long as they didn't have to invest any significant amount of money.

Peter told them they didn't need to worry about making any financial commitment. He planned to use the two hundred million dollars he got from the sale of his 20% of the shares towards the start-up costs of Wizard Computers.

They voted. Four slips of folded paper were tossed into a banker's box. Peter tallied the votes: *Yes. Yes. Yes. Yes.*

CHAPTER 47

The four co-owners of Wizard Computers arranged for the product to be manufactured and assembled by an overseas company. They agreed on this decision unanimously so their time could be freed up to run the daily operations. Although the cost of doing this was going to be high, not having the worries of running a factory would give them a tremendous amount of freedom.

Alex recommended an overseas company called *Po Industries*. It was located in the city of Haipai. The owner of Po Industries was a young businessman named Len Po.

Len Po was thirty-seven years old and had been in the manufacturing business for twenty-five years. He had an MBA and a degree in Industrial Design. His wife, Lia Po, was thirty-four years old. She was the head of the finance department for their jointly-owned company. She also had an MBA as well as a bachelor degree in Accounting. Between the two of them, they made all the important decisions for Po Industries.

It was decided that parties from both companies should meet at Po Industries headquarters to sign the contract between them. This would officially begin their business arrangement. It would also give them a chance to forge a relationship since they would be working closely together in the production of The Wizard computers.

Alex and Peter flew to Haipai for the meeting. They caught an overnight international flight out of Bayport and slept most of the way in their business-class seats near the front of the jet. Twelve hours later they arrived at their destination. It was early evening, Haipai time.

As soon as they disembarked from the plane, they looked for their contact by the baggage area. Peter was glad he had pre-arranged a limousine service to escort them around.

"Wow is it hot!" Alex said as he took off his jacket and gazed around the Haipai airport. "It must be a *thousand* degrees in the shade!"

"Easily," remarked Peter. "Here's our driver." He pointed to a man dressed in a chauffeur's uniform holding up a sign that read PRESTON in black letters.

Soon the two men were whisked off to their hotel. Along the way they discussed their up-coming meeting with Po Industries. "I sure hope this is the right decision, Alex. A big chunk of our money is going into financing this production."

"It is. It is." Alex reassured Peter. The truth was he wasn't sure at all. "Len Po has an excellent reputation for being a reliable businessman. If it works out, we won't ever have to worry about the manufacturing part of the business. It will be a big weight off our shoulders."

Peter glanced at his business colleague. "Yes, you're right."

Soon the limousine drove up a steep driveway to the front entrance of a lavish hotel. A brass sign read: PALACE HOTEL; *palace* being the operative word. The entrance was bordered with a hedge of bougainvillea flowers. In the center of the circular driveway was a sixty-foot palm tree whose graceful branches swayed to and fro.

Peter paid the driver and arranged for him to meet them again the next morning at nine o'clock.

Alex and Peter walked into the hotel. The lobby of the Palace Hotel simulated a tropical garden. In the center were a miniature waterfall and a pool filled with giant goldfish. There were hanging tropical plants everywhere laden with exotic blossoms of every shape and color. Some were scented with a perfume that filled the lobby entrance.

The two men approached the front desk and were greeted by a male front-desk clerk with dark-rimmed glasses. He spoke English with only a slight trace of an accent. "Good evening. How may I help you?"

Peter smiled and replied, "Good evening. We have a reservation for a three-night stay under the name of *Preston*. P-R-E-S-T-O-N."

The clerk tapped in the name on a keyboard hidden from view. "Ah yes. Preston. Room #910. There are two bedrooms in this suite and a view of the harbor. Would you be so kind as to fill out our guest card. I will also need your credit card." He slipped a crisp white form in front of Peter and handed him an expensive pen with the name of the hotel etched in gold letters.

In a flourish Peter filled out the card and handed it back to the clerk along with his VISA Card. A moment later the clerk returned Peter's credit card, gave him a receipt, and the room swipe card. He also gave him a brochure describing the services of the hotel.

Off to the right of the lobby were a dining room and a bar-lounge. At that moment there were only a handful of guests in the lounge. "Let's get a drink later," Alex suggested. "Right now, I need a shower."

They took the elevator up to the ninth floor. When they arrived at Room 910, Peter unlocked the door with a swipe of the key card.

The suite did indeed have a wonderful view of the ocean. There was a glass-enclosed balcony with a table in the center. There were two bedrooms, a living room with a 54-inch plasma TV, a kitchenette, and two bathrooms. It was lavishly furnished with every convenience of a five-star hotel.

Peter chose one of the bedrooms and thankfully dropped his suitcase onto the bed. It had been a long trip and he was beginning to feel the affects of jet-lag. He quickly unpacked and headed for the shower.

*   *   *

After a good night's sleep, Peter and Alex got ready for their big meeting the next morning. The limousine arrived precisely at 9:00 A.M. Soon they were on their way to the headquarters of Po Industries.

It took forty-five minutes to make the journey. They traveled through busy streets until they reached the outskirts of Haipai. When they caught the freeway, they made good time getting to the industrial area of the city. Upon arrival, Peter arranged for the limousine to come back at three o'clock in the afternoon.

Po Industries was a manufacturing facility built on twenty-five acres of industrial-zoned land. It was huge. No, *monstrous* would be a better word to describe it. There were buildings sprawled over the property each performing a crucial part of the production process.

Alex and Peter followed signs to the Main Office. They soon found themselves in a reception area that was even more prestigious than their marketing office in Bayport. Peter announced to the receptionist that he had a meeting with Len Po at ten o'clock. He gave her his business card.

The receptionist made a quick call and said, "Someone will be here shortly to take you to the meeting. Would you like to have seat while you are waiting." She ushered the gentlemen to a sofa beneath a palm plant.

It was Len Po himself who arrived five minutes later. He introduced himself and shook hands with Alex and Peter. He led the way to a conference room on the second floor. Here there were five more people waiting, including Lia Po. Len introduced everyone and they all took their seats.

The new business partners spent the morning arranging for the production of The Wizard computers. Po Industries would be responsible for manufacturing the parts, assembling the product, testing each one, and then shipping the computers to a warehouse in Bayport.

Len Po recommended Saganay Shipping Co. to do the shipping. They offered excellent freight rates and operated out of the Haipai harbor. Peter was not familiar with the reputation of shipping companies so willing agreed to give them a try.

The arrangement called for the manufacturing of five million computers per signed contract. This arrangement was made to the satisfaction of all concerned parties.

Len Po was eager to do business but he was also cautious with the two strangers. *Will they try to cheat me?* Len wondered to himself. It wouldn't be the first time. His business was difficult enough as it was but when customers didn't pay, or didn't pay on time, it gave him headaches he didn't need to have.

Peter seemed to read Len's mind. Opening his briefcase he pulled out a white sealed envelope. He handed it to Len with a smile.

"Here's the deposit I promised you, Len. Fifty million dollars. It's a certified cheque, so you should have no trouble depositing it in your bank account."

Len's eyes lit up when he took the envelope and discreetly slipped it into his jacket pocket. "Very good, Mr. Preston. Now we can commence with the operation. Would you and Mr. Wiley like a tour of our facilities?"

Both men said, "Yes".

* * *

Po Industries made many products for companies all around the world. It used a variety of robotics and factory automation systems. There was at least one billion dollars worth of equipment throughout the facility. The company guaranteed competitive prices, top-quality merchandise, and had excellent working conditions for its employees. Believe it or not, this latter quality was often the one that convinced new business owners to give Po Industries a try.

The first thing Peter noticed when they entered the industrial facility was how clean it was. Even the floors shone in spite of the traffic they must receive. All the workers wore white uniforms and appeared to be healthy and strong. They were also polite. Several of the workers greeted the group of visitors with a friendly bow.

Len showed them a sample product that was currently being made by the Po facility. He explained the process it would take to manufacture the Wizard computers. First a prototype had to be made, and then once the manufacturing system was in place, the product would then be mass-produced.

Alex and Peter were impressed.

Len explained that the robots that did most of the assembly work. They were faster and more accurate than human workers. They could make things, sort things, and fit things together. They could even test things. Robots were really the true wonders of technology.

By the time they finished the tour, one hour later, Alex and Peter were confident in their choice of manufacturers. Len, too, felt more at ease now that he had met his new clients and the financing had been completed.

Len chatted freely to his new business friends giving them facts about how their product would be made and the costs involved in doing this.

* * *

The next day Peter and Alex flew home.

CHAPTER 48

Six months after its release, The Wizard was nominated for its first award. It had been selected from hundreds of commercial hi-tech products as a potential winner of the *Best Technology Design* award. This award would be presented by the Inventor's Club at the annual *Gizmos Awards* ceremony held at Gora Falls Resort on April 7th.

To prepare for this elite ceremony, Peter and Alex were being custom-fitted for suits at an expensive men's haberdashery in downtown Bayport. Facing a triangular full-length mirror, their measurements were being taken by a discreet clerk. Peter and Alex were discussing the up-coming event.

"Isn't it terrific about the nomination?" Peter said to Alex.

"Yes. And I think we deserve it too. Those Wizard computers are really sensational."

"Is Julie coming to the ceremony?" Peter asked casually via the reflection in the mirror.

"Yes she is. She's as thrilled as I am. Imagine what will happen if we win this award. It's going to be great for the business. Have you ever been to a Gizmos Awards ceremony before, Peter?"

"Once. Seven years ago. I went with a colleague from Dale University. One of our fellow professors was being nominated for the *Industrial Design* award. He didn't get it though. There's a lot of stiff competition for those awards."

"I'll bet there is. What was it like ... the ceremony?" Alex prodded.

Peter turned to face Alex. "The time I went it was packed. There must have been five hundred people there. Only it wasn't held at the Gora Falls Resort then; it was held at the Diamond Hotel, here in Bayport."

"Was it televised?" Alex asked.

"Not that time. But this time it will be. If I remember correctly from the brochure I received, the Innovations Channel will be broadcasting the show live."

"What's the anticipated attendance for this year's ceremony?" Alex kept the banter up for details.

"A thousand. At least I know our table is guaranteed eight guests." Peter chuckled.

"Let's hope the ceremony gets lots of publicity," Alex said optimistically.

"The Gizmos Awards is one of the most prestigious awards ceremonies. They always get a lot of publicity," Peter assured Alex.

After the measurements for the suits were taken and written down in pencil on a white pad of paper, Peter and Alex were asked to select the colors and style. Peter chose grey-green cashmere, the color of "kimberlite" which is a volcanic rock that sometimes contains diamonds. Alex chose indigo because he believed the color purple signified intelligence.

Before departing each man paid a thousand-dollar deposit for their custom-made suits. They would pay the balance when their suits were finished.

"They'll be ready next Friday," announced the pleased owner of *The Gentry Shop.*

"Good," said Peter as he folded and tucked his receipt away. "I'll come by in the afternoon."

CHAPTER 49

Gora Falls Resort was a mammoth facility built adjacent to Gora Falls. The resort had a 1000-room hotel, a casino, a golf course, a shopping mall, and a racetrack. On active duty throughout the day were eight hundred employees serving the whims of their guests. Most of the rooms had a view of the falls. The sound of the roaring water could be heard from every balcony.

The Gizmos Awards ceremony was to be held in the main ballroom of the hotel. It was large enough to seat fifteen hundred guests. The room was elegant with chandeliers, high ceilings, an entertainment platform, and had a black-and-white checkered floor.

The ballroom was decorated for the event. Along the walls were mounted prints of past-winners of the Gizmos Awards and their corresponding achievements. Success story after success story told a history of twenty years of awards that had been won. After tonight's ceremony was over, these prints would be returned to the *Inventor's Club Museum* in Bayport.

Circular tables seating eight guests each were positioned throughout the immense room. The tables were covered with white linen tablecloths. In the centerpiece of each table was an electronic candle that had been designed by a former member of the Inventor's Club. The candles were touted as safe since they couldn't catch fire if they accidentally tipped over.

Each place-setting was laid out with the finest silverware and china provided by the resort's caterers. A white folded card with the guest's name in silver lettering sat in the center of each plate. There was a knife, a main fork, a desert fork, two spoons, a dinner plate, a side plate, a water glass, and a wine glass at each setting. There was a linen napkin folded in the shape of circular hat positioned on the side plate. The setting was poised for the pending gourmet dinner.

In dead center of the room was a raised platform with a podium and a microphone. It was here where the awards would be presented later in the evening. On this platform were six display stands each covered over with black velvet cloth. Underneath were the winning inventions that would later be revealed as the awards were presented. Around the platform area was a thick red rope held up by brass stands. There were several "Do Not Enter" signs hanging from these ropes discouraging anyone from entering the platform before the ceremony.

There were three tables near the center-stage for VIP guests. These special seats were for the president of the Inventor's Club, three previous Gizmos Awards winners of now-famous inventions, the owner of the Gora Falls Resort, and a handful of representatives from the press. There was also a camera crew on hand ready to televise the event on Channel 89, the *Innovations Channel.*

The event called for formal attire. Each guest was required to present their invitation at the door to security staff to gain access to the room.

By six o'clock all the tables were filled to capacity. An exciting buzz permeated the atmosphere. Tonight was an important occasion. It would set the pace for things to come. Much was at stake in the Gizmos Awards and everyone there knew it. A winning design could make a company owner rich and famous overnight.

At Wizard Computer's table were eight guests: Peter Preston, Alex and Julie Wiley, Henri Larue, Melanie Gold, and three of the firm's top personnel. Each of them wore a silver pin etched with the logo and name of their company. Their table was about thirty feet away from the awards platform. Everyone at the table was pleased with the view they had.

"Isn't this a great spot?" Julie whispered into Alex's ear. She wore a black jumpsuit with a high collar and a wide silver buckled belt. Her hair was done in a French braid. Her makeup had been professionally administered by one of the staff of the resort's numerous spas. Around her neck Julie wore a necklace of rectangular sapphires that sparkled in the light from the overhead chandeliers. She kept her silver clutch purse nearby.

Alex nodded. "We've got one of the best views in the place."

The noise of the crowd was growing in intensity. It would soon be impossible to converse. Julie put one hand over her husbands and squeezed it. Her excitement went through him like a small electrical charge.

Henri Larue sat between Julie and Melanie and declared it was the best place to be even though his back was to the stage. He joked with everyone at the table. He was in a terrific mood. Melanie spoke to him in French which pleased him to no end. Attending the Gizmos Awards ceremony was a highlight in Henri's non-stop career of accomplishments. He could proudly place another notch in his tree of success stories. Even if they didn't win, just being nominated was a sign of achievement to him.

Peter's eyes were scanning the crowd looking for people he knew. Over the past few years he had become adept at "networking" which invariably brought in more business. He spotted three people he recognized and made a mental note to speak with them after the ceremony was over.

*   *   *

At 6:15 p.m. the dinner began. Rex Morgan was the current president of the Inventor's Club and the host for tonight's ceremony. Rex was a handsome man, over six feet tall with broad shoulders, and a natural grace. He was a charming crowd-pleaser which made him the perfect host. His blond hair was neatly cut, gelled, and brushed back from his face.

"Good evening everyone." Rex's voice boomed over the microphone as he tapped it to make sure it was working. There were no squeals in this deluxe digital system. Soon Rex had all the guests' attention.

"Welcome to the *20th Annual Gizmos Awards!*"

The crowd burst into applause. Whistles could be heard throughout the ballroom.

"My name is Rex Morgan and I will be your host for the ceremony. We have a very special evening planned for you tonight. I want you all to enjoy it. I know I will."

Another round of applause swept throughout the room as Rex gave his introductory speech. "We're going to begin with a scrumptious dinner that has been prepared for us by the resort's catering chef, André Savant. After the dinner is over, we will be announcing this year's winners of the Gizmos Awards. The ceremony will be televised live by Channel 89 beginning exactly at eight o'clock. Following the awards there will be a social get-together until midnight.

"So ... eat ... drink ... and enjoy. The night is going to be full of surprises!"

Rex signaled the hotel catering staff, lined up along the wall of the ballroom, to begin serving dinner.

Since the Inventor's Club was sponsoring the dinner, it was decided that *brain food* would be the focus of the meal because inventors and designers were considered the smartest people on the planet. The main entrée included: shrimp paté, salmon steaks, jasmine rice, baby carrots, spinach salad, and fresh buns. For dessert there was a fruit trifle soaked in brandy.

In the center of each table was a bottle of ice-wine resting in a silver bucket filled with shaved ice. The wine created much talk amongst the guests about how ice-wine was made. The grapes were allowed to be frozen and then picked in the middle of the night. The flavor of the fresh grape was forever captured in the wine and not lost through processing or time. Hence, the name: *ice-wine*.

At seven-thirty the tables were cleared and prepared for the awards presentation. The guests sipped their coffee and liqueurs while watching the stage.

At two minutes to eight, Rex Morgan bounded up onto the stage. A young woman in her early twenties accompanied him. She would be his assistant during the ceremony. She wore a black velvet evening gown, long elbow-length black gloves, with diamonds dripping from her throat, wrist, and fingers. She stood in the center of the stage while Rex took his place at the podium.

The cameras began. A bright light shone on Rex while he spoke. The guests became quiet and tense with anticipation.

"Ladies and gentlemen. This is the moment we have all been waiting for. It is now time to announce this year's winners of the 20th annual Gizmos Awards. These awards will be given only to the most exceptional inventors and designers. The winners have been carefully chosen by our panel of ten judges. These judges, by the way, are all members of the Inventor's Club and are inventors themselves.

"Each year, in the past, we choose a winner from five separate categories. Well this year I am pleased to announce we have added a sixth category. So there will be six gizmos given away tonight to six talented designers."

The guests applauded this announcement.

The assistant came forward and handed Rex a large box. He reached inside and pulled out a sealed envelope. "Our first award will be given to the winner for *Best Industrial Design* ... from a list of five nominees." Rex opened the envelope and pulled out a silver-embossed card. He read the name. "The winner is ... *Aqua Robotics* ... for their design of the underwater robotic assembler."

The crowd clapped and cheered while the assistant went over to one of the display stands and removed a black cloth. Underneath was a miniature model of the robotic assembler sitting on a pedestal.

A representative from Aqua Robotics came onto the stage. He shook the host's hand. Rex handed him a small statue of a light bulb. The light bulb was the theme of the Gizmos Awards because it symbolized an "idea" as the beginning stage of all inventions. The statue was made of solid white platinum and stood about five inches tall. At the base of the statue were details about the winner of the award.

Rex handed the winner a plain envelope. "On behalf of the Inventor's Club, I would like to present you with a cheque for twenty-five thousand dollars, to be used towards your next industrial design. We hope one day it will be a winner too."

"Thank you!" the representative said in a pleased voice as he took the cheque from Rex. He held up the award high with his right hand and waved it in the air. The crowd clapped and cheered loudly as the representative from Aqua Robotics departed the stage. Rex reached into the box and pulled out another envelope. "Our second award goes to the inventor of *Best Consumer Product* from a list of five nominees." Rex opened the envelope, pulled out the card, and read the name. "The winner is ... *My Travel Company* ... for their design of the *Buzz* business travel case."

Since many of the guests were already familiar with the Buzz travel case they clapped even louder for this award winner. Rex's assistant removed the black cloth from one of the displays to reveal a sample of the Buzz travel case sitting on a pedestal.

A young man in his mid-twenties came onto the stage to accept the award. He gave a small speech thanking the staff in his company for assisting in the development of the product. He waved when he left the stage.

Rex pulled out another envelope from the box. "Our third award goes to the inventor of *Best Technology Design* from a list of five nominees." Rex opened the envelope and pulled out the silver-embossed card. He read the name. "The winner is ... *Wizard Computers* ... for their design of the online search computer called *The Wizard*."

The crowd clapped and cheered. Rex's assistant removed the black cloth from one of the display stands to reveal a model of The Wizard sitting on a pedestal.

Julie Wiley walked graciously onto the stage to receive the award. She kissed Rex on the cheek. On behalf of Wizard Computers she promised they would always treasure the award. She took the cheque for twenty-five thousand dollars to be used towards their next technology design. Waving to the crowd, Julie made her way back to her table.

* * *

After the awards ceremony was over many guests milled around Wizard Computer's table to offer their congratulations. Peter shook hands with as many people as he could and introduced them to the other members of the design team. Their gizmos award sat proudly in the center of their table. Engraved on the front were the words:

Best Technology Design

WIZARD COMPUTERS

20th Annual Gizmos Awards

Presented by the Inventor's Club

The statue was a symbol of their achievement. The award had elevated their company to a higher platform.

Rex Morgan made his way over to their table and shook hands with everyone. "On behalf of the Inventor's Club, I would like to offer my personal congratulations on your fine achievement." He asked the team members to drop by the next morning in Conference Room A where there would be a professional photo session of all the winners. These photos would later be published in the next issue of *Dezine,* a monthly magazine put out by the Inventor's Club. With a subscription base of more than one million subscribers, as well as an online version to countless viewers, the awards article would provide extensive publicity.

Rex explained to them this kind of exposure could escalate their company's sales. "You better get ready for it," he teased the team from Wizard Computers. "You're going to get calls coming out your ears. Winning this award will send you all the way to the top!"

With a smile, Rex disappeared into the crowd.

CHAPTER 50

A full moon over the Cactus Desert looked like a ghost wandering across the sky. It didn't brighten up the night at all. It just turned the landscape into iridescent shades of gray.

At the original Oro mine site, thousands of bats began emerging from the abandoned tunnel and flying out into the night, darting here and there in a flight pattern that was haphazard and unpredictable. They went in search of food: mosquitoes, moths, and bugs. They were like blind birds following built-in radar to keep them from running into things. No human needed to be warned; the fear of bats was instinctive. Bats often carried rabies, a deadly disease that didn't just kill its victims, it made them go insane first.

Two miles west of the Oro mine site was the manufacturing facility for the DIMKEL computers. Built only yards away from the desert, it was often the target of nightly bat raids. It wasn't unusual to see hundreds of bats circling the building in the wee hours of the night. That is, of course, if a person dared to wonder around in the dark to have a look at them.

The DIMKEL factory operated twenty-four hours a day, seven days a week. It produced 50,000 units every single day. It was a good thing they did, because business was growing daily. The demand for DIMKEL computers continued to increase at a steady rate.

Inside the manufacturing facility, in his lonely office, sat George Peppard reading an article about the recent Gizmos Awards ceremony he had come across it while flipping through a recent issue of *Dezines*. He learned of the success of The Wizard computer, designed by his former boss, Peter Preston, and DIM's original design team.

George read in detail who each of the Gizmos Awards winners were and what inventions were chosen. Since George knew nothing of The Wizard computers, until reading this article, he was surprised and pleased to hear that Peter was back in business again. At the back of his mind, he mildly wondered if Drekkel knew about The Wizard.

*　*　*

The board of directors for Drekkel Corporation met on the first Monday of every month in the Executive's Lounge on the fifth floor. There were ten members including Dick Drekkel, the CEO.

Coincidentally, on this particular Monday morning, the board was discussing the impact The Wizard computers were having on their business.   Roger Thornton, Vice-president of Operations, was concerned that these new computers would put sales of the DIMKEL computers into a slump.   "According to our research, the sales of Wizard computers now exceed the sales of DIMKEL computers by a 3% margin.   If this is the sign of a trend, our company is going to be in trouble.   We've gotta do something about it.   We've invested a lot of money into our manufacturing facility.   It would be a disaster if it failed now.   We are nowhere near paying off our investors on this project!"   Roger was clearly angry with this unforeseen development.

When Dick Drekkel first heard about The Wizard computers he was only slightly annoyed.   So someone was making a clone of his product.   So what!   It wasn't as if that was illegal.   He was no fool.   He knew clones were a part of big business.   He would be the last person to speak against the principles of cloning.

Ignoring Roger, Drekkel addressed the other board members. "I disagree!   This clone company isn't going to stop the sales of DIMKEL computers.   If anything, I bet it will help *increase* our sales.   It is a commonly known fact that competition is good for business."

Did he really believe that?

Roger Thornton didn't want to go up against Drekkel on this matter.   But neither did he want to sit back idly and watch the axe fall on their company.   He raised his hands in the air.   "Don't say I didn't warn you!"

Dick Drekkel reassured the other board members that DIMKEL was doing well. Since it had started, twelve months ago, the sales had increased to the point they were now averaging production of about 48,000 units a day. *Hey, that wasn't too shabby.* "Let's keep our eyes on the ball, shall we. Let's not worry about what other companies are doing. DIMKEL sales are going up all the time. That's all that we need to be concerned about." The other board members reluctantly agreed.

And that ended that discussion.

*   *   *

Veronica Hill looked up from her desk as a deliveryman leaned against the other side of the reception counter. "Can I help you?" she inquired.

The man in a brown uniform glanced over his clipboard. "I got a delivery here for someone named Richard Orem Drekkel. It's kind of big though. Where would you like me to put it?"

Veronica came around from behind the receptionist desk to inspect the package sitting on a dolly. It was a box about three feet wide and two feet high. There were no labels on the box. She became curious. "Who's it from?"

The deliveryman glanced at the sheet on his clipboard again. "Umm ... it says here it's from ... Research Technologies." He gave a shrug of his shoulders as if to say he didn't know anything more about it.

Her boss hadn't mentioned a delivery. But then he had been keeping a lot of things from her lately. Maybe it just slipped his mind.

"I'll show you where you can put it." Veronica led the deliveryman to Drekkel's vacant office. She instructed the deliveryman to put the box underneath the window. Then she signed for the delivery. The deliveryman left the office wheeling the empty dolly behind him.

*　　*　　*

At four o'clock that afternoon Drekkel returned to his office. It had been a hectic day and he felt tired and irritable. His mind was still on the board of directors meeting which frankly he thought hadn't gone all that well.

It was the first time he had been to his office all day. All he wanted to do was sit, relax, and read his mail. He needed some stress-free downtime.

As soon as Drekkel entered the office he saw the box sitting under the window. *What the hell is that?* He felt instantly annoyed, as though someone had purposely put it there just to bug him. He went over and inspected it. *No label.*

Drekkel stomped back over to his desk and pressed the intercom button with a jab of his index finger. "Veronica," he barked. "Would you get in here, please?"

A moment later Drekkel's trusty secretary slunk into his office as though she were trying to remain invisible.

"Close the door, will you!" Drekkel barked the order at her.

Veronica suddenly felt nervous. She knew from past experience that when her boss avoided eye contact he was usually in an unpredictable mood. "What's up?" she asked meekly.

"I want to know where that box came from." Drekkel pointed to the box in the corner. "There is no label on it." He stared accusingly at Veronica as though somehow it were her fault.

Was that all? Veronica let out a sigh of relief and went over to the box. She clipped the edge of the box with a long red-polished fingernail. "I don't know where it came from," she lied. "It was delivered this morning to you personally. Do you want me to open it?" When Veronica became peeved she became snippy.

"No!" Drekkel snapped. "I'll do it."

He went around behind his desk and yanked open the top drawer. He rummaged around and pulled out a pair of six-inch steel scissors. With them in hand he marched over to the box. He began cutting away strips of shipping tape that kept the box tightly bound.

When the lid of the box popped open, a flurry of Styrofoam chips spilled out onto the floor. Drekkel threw the scissors on the floor and began digging around the chips inside the box. He reached something hard. Not caring about the mess he was making, he pulled out the body of a computer.

Drekkel carried it over to a nearby table and set it down. He began inspecting the computer from all sides.

Veronica tiptoed over to the box. She pulled out a keyboard that was partially in view. There was an envelope taped to the front. "Oh look, Mr. Drekkel, there's an envelope here with your name on it." She set the keyboard down beside the computer. Using her fingernail she pried off the envelope.

Veronica went over to Drekkel's desk and found a letter-opener in his pencil holder that was in the shape of sword encrusted with phony gems on the handle. She inserted the tip of the letter-opener into the corner of the envelope and sliced it open with the sweep of her hand. She was good at doing this.

Inside was a 4" X 4" card. Veronica pulled it out. She was about to hand it to her boss when she heard him bellow, *"Greenvale?!"*

Drekkel was looking at the back of the computer where he had discovered a metal label. It read: *WIZARD COMPUTERS, Greenvale, Hidden Valley District.*

"The head office for Wizard Computers is in *Greenvale?*" Drekkel's face went a deep shade of red. He angrily faced his nervous secretary. "Do you know what this means, Veronica?"

Veronica went pale at the sight of his mounting rage and shook her head dumbly. She crept around the back of the desk to put some distance between the two of them. She didn't like the way he was looking at her.

"Greenvale?" she said weakly. "That means..." but Veronica didn't get a chance to finish her sentence.

Drekkel spun around and kicked the cardboard box. A cloud of Styrofoam chips flew into the air and landed all over the office floor.

"Give me that damned envelope!" Drekkel suddenly demanded.

Veronica went over to him clearly frightened and gingerly handed him the card. Drekkel snatched it from her and read it out loud: *"Compliments of Wizard Computers."*

In a fit a fury he tore the card into shreds and threw the pieces on the floor.

"When you're done cleaning up in here, Veronica, get me *Preston* on the phone!"

Drekkel stomped out of the office and slammed the door behind him.

CHAPTER 51

Peter got the call at his factory office. He wasn't surprised. In fact, he was expecting it. "Hello, Peter Preston here."

"This is Veronica Hill. I'm not sure if you remember me or not ... Mr. Preston, but I work for Drekkel Corporation."

Peter leaned back in his swivel chair and a smile spread slowly across his face. "Sure I remember you, Veronica." His voice poured like honey into Veronica's ears. "What can I do for you?"

"Mr. Drekkel would like to speak to you. It's important. Can you hold while I transfer the call?" Veronica did her best not to sound like she was desperate even though she knew she was. What would happen to her if she were not successful in making this connection?

"Go ahead, Veronica," said Peter smoothly.

"Thank you, Mr. Preston." Veronica quickly transferred the call.

A few seconds later Drekkel came on the line. "Preston!" he barked rudely into the phone. "This is Richard Orem Drekkel here!" Before Peter could reply, Drekkel continued. "I don't know what kind of a game you think you are playing with me Preston ... but you're not going to get away with it." His voice became fierce and deadly. "You took *my* money and used it to start this new company of yours ... Wizard Computers, didn't you? You lied to me, Preston. Why didn't you mention this new computer during our negotiations? It is obviously a modification of the DIM computer. And that means it belongs to *me*! This is the most dishonest thing that anyone has ever done. I'm going to report you to the Securities Exchange Commission and then I am going to ruin you publicly. Every person in the whole goddamned country is going to know what a lowdown businessman you are. And then I'm going to sue your ass to kingdom come! When I get finished with you, you won't be able to run a lemonade stand at the Greenvale Farmer's Market. I know my rights, Preston, and I am going to exercise them to the fullest. You'll be sorry..."

Peter had heard enough. He had regretted doing business with Drekkel from the moment he agreed to sell his shares in the takeover. Would he ever forget what it felt like losing his company? Drekkel could go to hell. He wasn't going to be intimidated by him any longer. In an equally loud voice, Peter barked back into the phone, "What's the matter, Drekkel? Afraid of a little competition?!!!"

For a minute there was dead silence. And then Peter began to laugh. All the tension from the takeover dissolved and he couldn't stop himself. He laughed so hard he dropped the phone over the side of his desk. He laughed until his sides hurt. Thinking about the fast one he had pulled on Drekkel made him laugh even more. Yes, he *had* deliberately used Drekkel's money to fund a company that would ultimately put his opponent out of business. But did Peter care? No, he did not. Wizard Computers was going to beat DIMKEL and Drekkel might end up bankrupt. So what? That was too bad. Shit happens!

It was a good five minutes later when Peter finally got a hold over himself. He had to grip his desk to keep himself steady. He reached over and picked up the phone. He listened but all he could hear was the sound of an automated recording: "... please hang up and try your call again ... this is a recording ... please hang up and try your call again ... this is a recording ..."

Drekkel had obviously hung up on him.

Oh well.